I0541318

Comic Tragedies

Louisa May Alcott &
Anna Alcott Pratt

Comic Tragedies

Copyright © 2020 Bibliotech Press
All rights reserved

The present edition is a reproduction of previous publication of this classic work. Minor typographical errors may have been corrected without note; however, for an authentic reading experience the spelling, punctuation, and capitalization have been retained from the original text.

ISBN: 978-1-63637-050-7

CONTENTS

A FOREWORD BY MEG

In the good old times, when "Little Women" worked and played together, the big garret was the scene of many dramatic revels. After a long day of teaching, sewing, and "helping mother," the greatest delight of the girls was to transform themselves into queens, knights, and cavaliers of high degree, and ascend into a world of fancy and romance. Cinderella's godmother waved her wand, and the dismal room became a fairy-land. Flowers bloomed, forests arose, music sounded, and lovers exchanged their vows by moonlight. Nothing was too ambitious to attempt; armor, gondolas, harps, towers, and palaces grew as if by magic, and wonderful scenes of valor and devotion were enacted before admiring audiences.

Jo, of course, played the villains, ghosts, bandits, and disdainful queens; for her tragedy-loving soul delighted in the lurid parts, and no drama was perfect in her eyes without a touch of the demonic or supernatural. Meg loved the sentimental rôles, the tender maiden with the airy robes and flowing locks, who made impossible sacrifices for ideal lovers, or the cavalier, singing soft serenades and performing lofty acts of gallantry and prowess. Amy was the fairy sprite, while Beth enacted the page or messenger when the scene required their aid.

But the most surprising part of the performance was the length of the cast and the size of the company; for Jo and Meg usually acted the whole play, each often assuming five or six characters, and with rapid change of dress becoming, in one scene, a witch, a soldier, a beauteous lady, and a haughty noble. This peculiar arrangement accounts for many queer devices, and the somewhat singular fact that each scene offers but two actors, who vanish and reappear at most inopportune moments, and in a great variety of costume. Long speeches were introduced to allow a ruffian to become a priest, or a lovely damsel to disguise herself in the garb of a sorceress; while great skill was required to preserve the illusion, and astonish the audience by these wonderful transformations.

The young amateur of to-day, who can easily call to her aid all the arts of the costumer and scene-maker, will find it hard to understand the difficulties of this little company; for not only did they compose their plays, but they were also their own carpenters, scene-painters, property-men, dress-makers, and managers. In place of a well-appointed stage, with the brilliant lights and inspiring accessories of a mimic theatre, the "Little Women" had a gloomy garret or empty barn, and were obliged to exercise all their ingenuity to present the scenes of their ambitious dramas.

But it is surprising what fine effects can be produced with old sheets, bright draperies, and a judicious arrangement of lights, garlands, and picturesque properties; and Jo's dramatic taste made her an admirable stage-manager. Meg was especially handy with saw and hammer, and acted as stage-carpenter,—building balconies, thrones, boats, and towers after peculiar designs of her own. Bureaus, tables, and chairs, piled aloft and arched with dark shawls, made dungeon walls and witch's cave, or formed a background for haunted forest and lonely glen. Screens of white cloth furnished canvas on which little Amy's skilful hand depicted palace halls, or romantic scene for lovers' tryst; and Beth's deft fingers were most apt in constructing properties for stage adornment, and transforming the frailest material into dazzling raiment. For the costumes were a serious consideration. No money could be spared from the slender purse to supply the wardrobes of these aspiring actors, and many were the devices to clothe the little company.

Thus a robe in one scene became a cloak in the next, and the drapery of a couch in the third; while a bit of lace served as mantle, veil, or turban, as best suited the turn of the play. Hats covered with old velvet, and adorned with feathers plucked from the duster, made most effective headgear for gay cavalier or tragic villain. From colored cotton were manufactured fine Greek tunics and flowing trains; and remarkable court costumes were evolved from an old sofa-covering, which had seen better days, and boasted a little gold thread and embroidery.

Stars of tin, sewed upon dark cambric, made a suit of shining armor. Sandals were cut from old boots. Strips of wood and silver paper were fashioned into daggers, swords, and spears, while from cardboard were created helmets, harps, guitars, and antique lamps, that were considered masterpieces of stage art.

Everything available was pressed into service; colored paper, odds and ends of ribbon, even tin cans and their bright wrappings were treasures to the young actors, and all reappeared as splendid properties.

At first a store of red curtains, some faded brocades, and ancient shawls comprised the stage wardrobe; but as the fame of the performances spread abroad, contributions were made to the little stock, and the girls became the proud possessors of a velvet robe, a plumed hat adorned with silver, long yellow boots, and a quantity of mock pearls and tinsel ornaments.

Such wealth determined them to write a play which should surpass all former efforts, give Jo a chance to stalk haughtily upon the stage in the magnificent boots, and Meg to appear in gorgeous train and diadem of jewels.

"The Witch's Curse" was the result, and it was produced with astounding effect, quite paralyzing the audience by its splendid gloom. Jo called it the "lurid drama," and always considered it her masterpiece. But it cost hours of thought and labor; for to construct a dungeon, a haunted chamber, a cavern, and a lonely forest taxed to the uttermost the ingenuity of the actors. To introduce into one short scene a bandit, two cavaliers, a witch, and a fairy spirit—all enacted by two people—required some skill, and lightning change of costume. To call up the ghostly visions and mysterious voices which should appall the guilty Count Rodolpho, was a task of no small difficulty. But inspired by the desire to outshine themselves, the children accomplished a play full of revenge, jealousy, murder, and sorcery, of all which indeed they knew nothing but the name.

Hitherto their dramas had been of the most sentimental description, given to the portrayal of woman's devotion, filial affection, heroism, and self-sacrifice. Indeed, these "Comic Tragedies" with their highflown romance and fantastic ideas of love and honor, are most characteristic of the young girls whose lives were singularly free from the experiences of many maidens of their age.

Of the world they knew nothing; lovers were ideal beings, clothed with all the beauty of their innocent imaginations. Love was a blissful dream; constancy, truth, courage, and virtue quite every-day affairs of life. Their few novels furnished the romantic element; the favorite fairy-tales gave them material for the supernatural; and their strong dramatic taste enabled them to infuse both fire and pathos into their absurd situations.

Jo revelled in catastrophe, and the darker scenes were her delight; but she usually required Meg to "do the love-part," which she considered quite beneath her pen. Thus their productions were a queer mixture of sentiment and adventure, with entire disregard of such matters as grammar, history, and geography,—all of which were deemed of no importance by these aspiring dramatists.

From the little stage library, still extant, the following plays have been selected as fair examples of the work of these children of sixteen and seventeen. With some slight changes and omissions, they remain as written more than forty years ago by Meg and Jo, so dear to the hearts of many other "Little Women."

Concord, Mass., 1893

NORNA; OR, THE WITCH'S CURSE

CHARACTERS

Count *Rodolpho A Haughty Noble*.

Count *Louis Lover of Leonore*.

Adrian *The Black Mask*.

Hugo *A Bandit*.

Gaspard *Captain of the Guard*.

Angelo *A Page*.

Theresa *Wife to Rodolpho*.

Leonore *In love with Louis*.

Norna *A Witch*.

SCENE FIRST

[*A room in the castle of* Rodolpho. Theresa *discovered alone, and in tears.*]

Theresa. I cannot pray; my aching heart finds rest alone in tears. Ah, what a wretched fate is mine! Forced by a father's will to wed a stranger ere I learned to love, one short year hath taught me what a bitter thing it is to wear a chain that binds me unto one who hath proved himself both jealous and unkind. The fair hopes I once cherished are now gone, and here a captive in my splendid home I dwell forsaken, sorrowing and alone [*weeps*]. [*Three taps upon the wall are heard.*] Ha, my brother's signal! What can bring him hither at this hour? Louis, is it thou? Enter; "all's well."

[*Enter* Count Louis *through a secret panel in the wall, hidden by a CURTAIN He embraces* Theresa.

Theresa. Ah, Louis, what hath chanced? Why art thou here? Some danger must have brought thee; tell me, dear brother. Let me serve thee.

Louis. Sister dearest, thy kindly offered aid is useless now. Thou canst not help me; and I must add another sorrow to the many that are thine. I came to say farewell, Theresa.

Theresa. Farewell! Oh, brother, do not leave me! Thy love is all now left to cheer my lonely life. Wherefore must thou go? Tell me, I beseech thee!

Louis. Forgive me if I grieve thee. I will tell thee all. Thy husband hates me, for I charged him with neglect and cruelty to thee; and he hath vowed revenge for my bold words. He hath whispered false tales to the king, he hath blighted all my hopes of rank and honor. I am banished from the land, and must leave thee and Leonore, and wander forth an outcast and alone. But—let him beware!—I shall return to take a deep revenge for thy wrongs and my own. Nay, sister, grieve not thus. I have sworn to free thee from his power, and I will keep my vow. Hope on and bear a little longer, dear Theresa, and ere long I will bear thee to a happy home [*noise is heard without*]. Ha! what is that? Who comes?

2

Theresa. 'Tis my lord returning from the court. Fly, Louis, fly! Thou art lost if he discover thee. Heaven bless and watch above thee. Remember poor Theresa, and farewell.

Louis. One last word of Leonore. I have never told my love, yet she hath smiled on me, and I should have won her hand. Ah, tell her this, and bid her to be true to him who in his exile will hope on, and yet return to claim the heart he hath loved so faithfully. Farewell, my sister. Despair not,—I shall return.

[*Exit* Louis *through the secret panel; drops his dagger.*

Theresa. Thank Heaven, he is safe!—but oh, my husband, this last deed of thine is hard to bear. Poor Louis, parted from Leonore, his fair hopes blighted, all by thy cruel hand. Ah, he comes! I must be calm.

[*Enter* Rodolpho.

Rod. What, weeping still? Hast thou no welcome for thy lord save tears and sighs? I'll send thee to a convent if thou art not more gay!

Theresa. I'll gladly go, my lord. I am weary of the world. Its gayeties but make my heart more sad.

Rod. Nay, then I will take thee to the court, and there thou *must* be gay. But I am weary; bring me wine, and smile upon me as thou used to do. Dost hear me? Weep no more. [*Seats himself.*] Theresa *brings wine and stands beside him. Suddenly he sees the dagger dropped by* Louis.] Ha! what is that? 'Tis none of mine. How came it hither? Answer, I command thee!

Theresa. I cannot. I must not, dare not tell thee.

Rod. Darest thou refuse to answer? Speak! Who hath dared to venture hither? Is it thy brother? As thou lovest life, I bid thee speak.

Theresa. I am innocent, and will not betray the only one now left me on the earth to love. Oh, pardon me, my lord; I will obey in all but this.

Rod. Thou *shalt* obey. I'll take thy life but I will know. Thy brother must be near,—this dagger was not here an hour ago. Thy terror hath betrayed him. I leave thee now to bid them search the castle.

But if I find him not, I shall return; and if thou wilt not then confess, I'll find a way to make thee. Remember, I have vowed,—thy secret or thy life!

[*Exit* Rodolpho.

Theresa. My life I freely yield thee, but my secret—never. Oh, Louis, I will gladly die to save thee. Life hath no joy for me; and in the grave this poor heart may forget the bitter sorrows it is burdened with [*sinks down weeping*].

[*Enter* Rodolpho.

Rod. The search is vain. He hath escaped. Theresa, rise, and answer me. To whom belonged the dagger I have found? Thy tears avail not; I will be obeyed. Kneel not to me, I will not pardon. Answer, or I swear I'll make thee dumb forever.

Theresa. No, no! I will not betray. Oh, husband, spare me! Let not the hand that led me to the altar be stained with blood I would so gladly shed for thee. I cannot answer thee.

Rod. [*striking her*]. Then die: thy constancy is useless. I will find thy brother and take a fearful vengeance yet.

Theresa. I am faithful to the last. Husband, I forgive thee.

[Theresa *dies*.

Rod. 'Tis done, and I am rid of her forever; but 'tis an ugly deed. Poor fool, there was a time when I could pity thee, but thou hast stood 'twixt me and Lady Leonore, and now I am free. I must conceal the form, and none shall ever know the crime.

[*Exit* Rodolpho.

[*The panel opens and* Norna *enters.*]

Norna. Heaven shield us! What is this? His cruel hand hath done the deed, and I am powerless to save. Poor, murdered lady, I had hoped to spare thee this, and lead thee to a happier home. Perchance, 'tis better so. The dead find rest, and thy sad heart can ache no more. Rest to thy soul, sweet lady. But for *thee*, thou cruel villain, I have in store a deep revenge for all thy sinful deeds. If there be power in spell or charm, I'll conjure fearful dreams upon thy head. I'll follow thee wherever thou mayst go, and haunt thy sleep with evil visions. I'll whisper strange words that shall appall thee; dark phantoms shall rise up before thee, and wild voices ringing in thine ear shall tell thee of thy sins. By all these will I make life like a hideous dream, and death more fearful still. Like a vengeful ghost I will haunt thee to thy grave, and so revenge thy wrongs, poor, murdered lady. Beware, Rodolpho! Old Norna's curse is on thee.

[*She bears away* Theresa's *body through the secret door, and vanishes.*

CURTAIN

NOTE TO SCENE SECOND

The mysterious cave was formed of old furniture, covered with dark draperies, an opening being left at the back wherein the spirits called up by Norna might appear. A kitchen kettle filled with steaming water made an effective caldron over which the sorceress should murmur her incantations; flaming pine-knots cast a lurid glare over the scene; and large boughs, artfully arranged about the stage, gave it the appearance of a "gloomy wood."

When Louis "retires within," he at once arrays himself in the white robes of the vision, and awaits the witch's call to rise behind the aperture in true dramatic style. He vanishes, quickly resumes his own attire, while Norna continues to weave her spells, till she sees he is ready to appear once more as the disguised Count Louis.

SCENE SECOND

[*A wood.* Norna's *cave among the rocks. Enter* Louis *masked.*]

Louis. Yes; 'tis the spot. How dark and still! She is not here. Ho, Norna, mighty sorceress! I seek thy aid.

Norna [*rising from the cave*]. I am here.

Louis. I seek thee, Norna, to learn tidings of one most dear to me. Dost thou know aught of Count Rodolpho's wife? A strange tale hath reached me that not many nights ago she disappeared, and none know whither she hath gone. Oh, tell me, is this true?

Norna. It is most true.

Louis. And canst thou tell me whither she hath gone? I will reward thee well.

Norna. I can. She lies within her tomb, in the chapel of the castle.

Louis. Dead!—it cannot be! They told me she had fled away with some young lord who had won her love. Was it not true?

Norna. It is false as the villain's heart who framed the tale. *I* bore the murdered lady to her tomb, and laid her there.

Louis. Murdered? How? When? By whom? Oh, tell me I beseech thee!

Norna. Her husband's cruel hand took the life he had made a burden. I heard him swear it ere he dealt the blow.

Louis. Wherefore did he kill her? Oh, answer quickly or I shall go mad with grief and hate.

Norna. I can tell thee little. From my hiding-place I heard her vow never to confess whose dagger had been found in her apartment, and her jealous lord, in his wild anger, murdered her.

Louis. 'Twas mine. Would it had been sheathed in mine own breast

7

ere it had caused so dark a deed! Ah, Theresa, why did I leave thee to a fate like this?

Norna. Young man, grieve not; it is too late to save, but there is left to thee a better thing than grief.

Louis. Oh, what?

Norna. Revenge!

Louis. Thou art right. I'll weep no more. Give me thine aid, O mighty wizard, and I will serve thee well.

Norna. Who art thou? The poor lady's lover?

Louis. Ah, no; far nearer and far deeper was the love I bore her, for I am her brother.

Norna. Ha, that's well! Thou wilt join me, for I have made a vow to rest not till that proud, sinful lord hath well atoned for this deep crime. Spirits shall haunt him, and the darkest phantoms that my art can raise shall scare his soul. Wilt thou join me in my work?

Louis. I will,—but stay! thou hast spoken of spirits. Dread sorceress, is it in thy power to call them up?

Norna. It is. Wilt see my skill. Stand back while I call up a phantom which thou canst not doubt.

[Louis *retires within the cave.* Norna *weaves a spell above her caldron.*

Norna. O spirit, from thy quiet tomb,
I bid thee hither through the gloom,
In winding-sheet, with bloody brow,
Rise up and hear our solemn vow.
I bid thee, with my magic power,
Tell the dark secret of that hour
When cruel hands, with blood and strife,
Closed the sad dream of thy young life.
Hither—appear before our eyes.
Pale spirit, I command thee *rise.*

[*Spirit of* Theresa *rises.*

Shadowy spirit, I charge thee well,

8

By my mystic art's most potent spell,
To haunt throughout his sinful life,
The mortal who once called thee wife.
At midnight hour glide round his bed,
And lay thy pale hand on his head.
Whisper wild words in his sleeping ear,
And chill his heart with a deadly fear.
Rise at his side in his gayest hour,
And his guilty soul shall feel thy power.
Stand thou before him in day and night,
And cast o'er his life a darksome blight;
For with all his power and sin and pride,
 He shall ne'er forget his murdered bride.
Pale, shadowy form, wilt thou obey?

[*The spirit bows its head.*

To thy ghostly work away—away!

[*The spirit vanishes.*

The spell is o'er, the vow is won,
And, sinful heart, *thy* curse begun.

[*Re-enter* Louis.

Louis. 'Tis enough! I own thy power, and by the spirit of my murdered sister I have looked upon, I swear to aid thee in thy dark work.

Norna. 'Tis well; and I will use my power to guard thee from the danger that surrounds thee. And now, farewell. Remember,—thou hast sworn.

[*Exit* Louis.

CURTAIN

SCENE THIRD

[*Another part of the wood. Enter* Rodolpho.]

Rod. They told me that old Norna's cave was 'mong these rocks, and yet I find it not. By her I hope to learn where young Count Louis is concealed. Once in my power, he shall not escape to whisper tales of evil deeds against me. Stay! some one comes. I'll ask my way.

[*Enter* Louis *masked.*

Ho, stand, good sir. Canst guide me to the cell of Norna, the old sorceress?

Louis. It were little use to tell thee; thou wouldst only win a deeper curse than that she hath already laid upon thee.

Rod. Hold! who art thou that dare to speak thus to Count Rodolpho?

Louis. That thou canst never know; but this I tell thee: I am thy deadliest foe, and, aided by the wizard Norna, seek to work thee evil, and bring down upon thy head the fearful doom thy sin deserves. Wouldst thou know more,—then seek the witch, and learn the hate she bears thee.

Rod. Fool! thinkst thou I fear thee or thy enchantments? Draw, and defend thyself! Thou shalt pay dearly for thine insolence to me! insolence to me!

[*Draws his sword.*

Louis. I will not stain my weapon with a murderer's blood. I leave thee to the fate that gathers round thee.

[*Exit* Louis.

Rod. "Murderer," said he. I am betrayed,—yet no one saw the deed. Yet, stay! perchance 'twas he who bore Theresa away. He has escaped me, and will spread the tale. Nay, why should I fear? Courage! One blow, and I am safe! [*Rushes forward. Spirit of* Theresa *rises.*] What's that?—her deathlike face,—the wound my hand hath made! Help! help! help!

[*Rushes out. The spirit vanishes.*

CURTAIN

SCENE FOURTH

[*Room in the castle of* Rodolpho. Rodolpho *alone.*]

Rod. I see no way save that. Were young Count Louis dead she would forget the love that had just begun, and by sweet words and gifts I may yet win her. The young lord must die [*a groan behind the curtain*]. Ha! what is that? 'Tis nothing; fie upon my fear! I'll banish all remembrance of the fearful shape my fancy conjured up within the forest. I'll not do the deed myself,—I have had enough of blood. Hugo the bandit: he is just the man,—bold, sure of hand, and secret. I will bribe him well, and when the deed is done, find means to rid me of him lest he should play me false. I saw him in the courtyard as I entered. Perchance he is not yet gone. Ho, without there! Bid Hugo here if he be within the castle.—He is a rough knave, but gold will make all sure.

[*Enter* Hugo.

Hugo. What would my lord with me?

Rod. I ask a favor of thee. Nay, never fear, I'll pay thee well. Wouldst earn a few gold pieces?

Hugo. Ay, my lord, most gladly would I.

Rod. Nay, sit, good Hugo. Here is wine; drink, and refresh thyself.

Hugo. Thanks, my lord. How can I serve you?

[Rodolpho *gives wine,* Hugo *sits and drinks.*]

Rod. Dost thou know Count Louis, whom the king lately banished?

Hugo. Nay, my lord; I never saw him.

Rod. [*aside*]. Ha! that is well. It matters not; 'tis not of him I speak. Take more wine, good Hugo. Listen, there is a certain lord,—one whom I hate. I seek his life. Here is gold—thou hast a dagger, and can use it well. Dost understand me?

Hugo. Ay, my lord, most clearly. Name the place and hour; count out the gold,—I and my dagger then are thine.

12

Rod. 'Tis well. Now harken. In the forest, near old Norna's cave, there is a quiet spot. Do thou go there to-night at sunset. Watch well, and when thou seest a tall figure wrapped in a dark cloak, and masked, spring forth, and do the deed. Then fling the body down the rocks, or hide it in some secret place. Here is one half the gold; more shall be thine when thou shalt show some token that the deed is done.

Hugo. Thanks, Count; I'll do thy bidding. At sunset in the forest,— I'll be there, and see he leaves it not alive. Good-even, then, my lord.

Rod. Hugo, use well thy dagger, and gold awaits thee. Yet, stay! I'll meet thee in the wood, and pay thee there. They might suspect if they should see thee here again so soon. I'll meet thee there, and so farewell.

Hugo. Adieu, my lord.

[*Exit* Hugo].

Rod. Yes; all goes well. My rival dead, and Leonore is mine. With her I may forget the pale face that now seems ever looking into mine. I can almost think the deep wound shows in her picture yonder. But this is folly! Shame on thee, Rodolpho. I'll think of it no more. [*Turns to drink.* Theresa's *face appears within the picture, the wound upon her brow.*] Ha! what is that? Am I going mad? See the eyes move,—it is Theresa's face! Nay, I will not look again. Yes, yes; 'tis there! Will this sad face haunt me forever?

Theresa. Forever! Forever!

Rod. Fiends take me,—'tis her voice! It is no dream. Ah, let me go away—away!

[Rodolpho *rushes wildly out.*]

CURTAIN

NOTE TO SCENE FIFTH

The apparently impossible transformations of this scene (when played by two actors only) may be thus explained:—

The costumes of Louis and Norna, being merely loose garments, afford opportunities for rapid change; and the indulgent audience overlooking such minor matters as boots and wigs, it became an easy matter for Jo to transform herself into either of the four characters which she assumed on this occasion.

Beneath the flowing robes of the sorceress Jo was fully dressed as Count Rodolpho. Laid conveniently near were the black cloak, hat, and mask of Louis,—also the white draperies required for the ghostly Theresa.

Thus, Norna appears in long, gray robe, to which are attached the hood and elf-locks of the witch. Seeing Hugo approach she conceals herself among the trees, thus gaining time to don the costume of Louis, and appear to Hugo who awaits him.

Hugo stabs and drags him from the stage. Louis then throws off his disguise and becomes Rodolpho, fully dressed for his entrance a moment later.

As Hugo does not again appear, it is an easy matter to assume the character of the spectre and produce the sights and sounds which terrify the guilty Count; then slipping on the witch's robe, be ready to glide forth and close the scene with dramatic effect.

SCENE FIFTH

[*The wood near* Norna's *cave. Enter* Norna.]

Norna. It is the hour I bid him come with the letter for Lady Leonore. Poor youth, his sister slain, his life in danger, and the lady of his love far from him, 'tis a bitter fate. But, if old Norna loses not her power, he shall yet win his liberty, his love, and his revenge. Ah, he comes,—nay, 'tis the ruffian Hugo. I will conceal myself,—some evil is afoot [*hides among the trees*].

[*Enter* Hugo.

Hugo. This is the spot. Here will I hide, and bide my time [*conceals himself among the rocks*].

[*Enter* Louis.

Louis. She is not here. I'll wait awhile and think of Leonore. How will she receive this letter? Ah, could she know how, 'mid all my grief and danger, her dear face shines in my heart, and cheers me on. [Hugo *steals out, and as he turns, stabs him.*] Ha, villain, thou hast killed me! I am dying! God bless thee, Leonore! Norna, remember, vengeance on Rodolpho! [*Falls*]

Hugo. Nay, nay, thou wilt take no revenge; thy days are ended, thanks to this good steel. Now, for the token [*takes letter from Louis's hand*]. Ah, this he cannot doubt. I will take this ring too; 'tis a costly one. I'll hide the body in the thicket yonder, ere my lord arrives [*drags out the body*].

[*Enter* Rodolpho.

Rod. Not here? Can he have failed? Here is blood—it may be his. I'll call. Hugo, good Hugo, art thou here?

Hugo [*stealing from the trees*]. Ay, my lord, I am here. All is safely done: the love-sick boy lies yonder in the thicket, dead as steel can make him. And here is the token if you doubt me, and the ring I just took from his hand [*gives letter*].

Rod. Nay, nay, I do not doubt thee; keep thou the ring. I am content

15

with this. Tell me, did he struggle with thee when thou dealt the blow?

Hugo. Nay, my lord; he fell without a groan, and murmuring something of revenge on thee, he died. Hast thou the gold?

Rod. Yes, yes, I have it. Take it, and remember I can take thy life as easily as thou hast his, if thou shouldst whisper what hath been this day done. Now go; I've done with thee.

Hugo. And I with thee. Adieu, my lord.

[*Exit* Hugo.

Rod. Now am I safe,—no mortal knows of Theresa's death by my hand, and Leonore is mine.

Voice [*within the wood*]. Never—never!

Rod. Curses on me! Am I bewitched? Surely, I heard a voice; perchance 'twas but an echo [*a wild laugh rings through the trees*]. Fiends take the wood! I'll stay no longer! [*Turns to fly*. Theresa's *spirit rises*.] 'Tis there,—help, help—[*Rushes wildly out*.]

[*Enter* Norna.

Norna. Ha, ha! fiends shall haunt thee, thou murderer! Another sin upon thy soul,—another life to be avenged! Poor, murdered youth, now gone to join thy sister. I will lay thee by her side and then to my work. He hath raised another ghost to haunt him. Let him beware!

[*Exit* Norna.

CURTAIN

SCENE SIXTH

[*Chamber in the castle of* Lady Leonore. *Enter* Leonore.]

Leonore. Ah, how wearily the days go by. No tidings of Count Louis, and Count Rodolpho urges on his suit so earnestly. I must accept his hand to-day, or refuse his love, and think no more of Louis. I know not how to choose. Rodolpho loves me: I am an orphan and alone, and in his lovely home I may be happy. I have heard it whispered that he is both stern and cruel, yet methinks it cannot be,—he is so tender when with me. Ah, would I could forget Count Louis! He hath never told his love, and doubtless thinks no more of her who treasures up his gentle words, and cannot banish them, even when another offers a heart and home few would refuse. How shall I answer Count Rodolpho when he comes? I do not love him as I should, and yet it were no hard task to learn with so fond a teacher. Shall I accept his love, or shall I reject?

[Norna *suddenly appears.*

Norna. Reject.

Leonore. Who art thou? Leave me, or I call for aid.

Norna. Nay, lady, fear not. I come not here to harm thee, but to save thee from a fate far worse than death. I am old Norna of the forest, and though they call me witch and sorceress, I am a woman yet, and with a heart to pity and to love. I would save thy youth and beauty from the blight I fear will fall upon thee.

Leonore. Save me! from what? How knowest thou I am in danger; and from what wouldst thou save me, Norna?

Norna. From Lord Rodolpho, lady.

Leonore. Ah! and why from him? Tell on, I'll listen to thee now. He hath offered me his heart and hand. Why should I not accept them, Norna?

Norna. That heart is filled with dark and evil passions, and that hand is stained with blood. Ay, lady, well mayst thou start. I will tell thee more. The splendid home he would lead thee to is darkened by

17

a fearful crime, and his fair palace haunted by the spirit of a murdered wife.

[Leonore *starts up.*

Leonore. Wife, sayest thou? He told me he was never wed. Mysterious woman, tell me more! How dost thou know 'tis true, and wherefore was it done? I have a right to know. Oh, speak, and tell me all!

Norna. For that have I come hither. He hath been wed to a lady, young and lovely as thyself. He kept her prisoner in his splendid home, and by neglect and cruelty he broke as warm and true a heart as ever beat in woman's breast. Her brother stole unseen to cheer and comfort her, and this aroused her lord's suspicions, and he bid her to confess who was her unknown friend. She would not yield her brother to his hate, and he in his wild anger murdered her. I heard his cruel words, her prayers for mercy, and I stood beside the lifeless form and marked the blow his evil hand had given her. And there I vowed I would avenge the deed, and for this have I come hither to warn thee of thy danger. He loves thee only for thy wealth, and when thou art his, will wrong thee as he hath the meek Theresa.

Leonore. How shall I ever thank thee for this escape from sorrow and despair? I did not love him, but I am alone, and his kind words were sweet and tender. I thought with him I might be happy yet, but—Ah, how little did I dream of sin like this! Thank Heaven, 'tis not too late!

Norna. How wilt thou answer Lord Rodolpho now?

Leonore. I will answer him with all the scorn and loathing that I feel. I fear him not, and he shall learn how his false vows are despised, and his sins made known.

Norna. 'Tis well; but stay,—be thou not too proud. Speak fairly, and reject him courteously; for he will stop at nought in his revenge if thou but rouse his hatred. And now, farewell. I'll watch above thee, and in thy hour of danger old Norna will be nigh. Stay, give me some token, by which thou wilt know the messenger I may find cause to send thee. The fierce Count will seek to win thee, and repay thy scorn by all the evil his cruel heart can bring.

Leonore. Take this ring, and I will trust whoever thou mayst send with it. I owe thee much, and, believe me, I am grateful for thy care, and will repay thee by my confidence and truth. Farewell, old

18

Norna; watch thou above the helpless, and thine old age shall be made happy by my care.

Norna. Heaven bless thee, gentle lady. Good angels guard thee. Norna will not forget.

[*Exit* Norna.

Leonore. 'Tis like a dream, so strange, so terrible,—he whom I thought so gentle, and so true is stained with fearful crimes! Poor, murdered lady! Have I escaped a fate like thine? Ah, I hear his step! Now, heart, be firm and he shall enter here no more.

[*Enter* Rodolpho.

Rod. Sweet lady, I am here to learn my fate. I have told my love, and thou hast listened; I have asked thy hand, and thou hast not refused it. I have offered all that I possess,—my home, my heart. Again I lay them at thy feet, beloved Leonore. Oh, wilt thou but accept them, poor tho' they be, and in return let me but claim this fair hand as mine own?

[*Takes her hand and kneels before her.*

Leonore [*withdrawing her hand*]. My lord, forgive me, but I cannot grant it. When last we met thou didst bid me ask my heart if it could love thee. It hath answered, "Nay." I grieve I cannot make a fit return for all you offer, but I have no love to give, and without it this poor hand were worthless. There are others far more fit to grace thy home than I. Go, win thyself a loving bride, and so forget Leonore.

Rod. What hath changed thee thus since last we met. Then wert thou kind, and listened gladly to my love. Now there is a scornful smile upon thy lips, and a proud light in thine eye. What means this? Why dost thou look so coldly on me, Leonore? Who has whispered false tales in thine ear? Believe them not. I am as true as Heaven to thee; then do not cast away the heart so truly thine. Smile on me, dearest; thou art my first, last, only love.

Leonore. 'Tis false, my lord! Hast thou so soon forgot *Theresa*?

Rod. What! Who told thee that accursed tale? What dost thou mean, Leonore?

Leonore. I mean thy sinful deeds are known. Thou hast asked me why I will not wed thee, and I answer, I will not give my hand unto a murderer.

19

Rod. Murderer! No more of this! Thy tale is false; forget it, and I will forgive the idle words. Now listen; I came hither to receive thy answer to my suit. Think ere thou decide. Thou art an orphan, unprotected and alone. I am powerful and great. Wilt thou take my love, and with it honor, wealth, happiness, and ease, or my hate, which will surely follow thee and bring down desolation on thee and all thou lovest? Now choose, my hatred, or my love.

Leonore. My lord, I scorn thy love, and I defy thy hate. Work thy will, I fear thee not. I am not so unprotected as thou thinkest. There are unseen friends around me who will save in every peril, and who are sworn to take revenge on thee for thy great sins. This is my answer; henceforth we are strangers; now leave me. I would be alone.

Rod. Not yet, proud lady. If thou wilt not love, I'll make thee learn to fear the heart thou hast so scornfully cast away. Let thy friends guard thee well; thou wilt need their care when I begin my work of vengeance. Thou mayst smile, but thou shalt rue the day when Count Rodolpho asked and was refused. But I will yet win thee, and then beware! And when thou dost pray for mercy on thy knees, remember the haughty words thou hast this day spoken.

Leonore. Do thy worst, murderer; spirits will watch above me, and thou canst not harm. Adieu, my lord.

[*Exit* Leonore.

Rod. Foiled again! Some demon works against me. Who could have told her of Theresa? A little longer, and I should have won a rich young bride, and now this tale of murder mars it all. But I will win her yet, and wring her proud heart till she shall bend her haughty head and sue for mercy.

How shall it be done? Stay! Ha, I see a way!—the letter Louis would have sent her ere he died. She knows not of his death, and I will send this paper bidding her to meet her lover in the forest. She cannot doubt the lines his own hand traced. She will obey,—and I'll be there to lead her to my castle. I'll wed her, and she may scorn, weep, and pray in vain. Ha, ha! proud Leonore, spite of thy guardian spirits thou shalt be mine, and then for my revenge!

[*Exit* Rodolpho.

CURTAIN

SCENE SEVENTH

[Leonore's *room. Enter* Leonore *with a letter.*]

Leonore. 'Tis strange; an unknown page thrust this into my hand while kneeling in the chapel. Ah, surely, I should know this hand! 'Tis Louis's, and at last he hath returned, and still remembers Leonore [*opens letter and reads*].

> Dearest Lady,—I am banished from the land by Count Rodolpho's false tales to the king; and thus I dare not venture near thee. But by the love my lips have never told, I do conjure thee to bestow one last look, last word, on him whose cruel fate it is to leave all that he most fondly loves. If thou wilt grant this prayer, meet me at twilight in the glen beside old Norna's cave. She will be there to guard thee. Dearest Leonore, before we part, perchance forever, grant this last boon to one who in banishment, in grief and peril, is forever thy devoted
>
> Louis.

He loves me, and mid danger still remembers. Ah, Louis, there is nothing thou canst ask I will not gladly grant. I'll go; the sun is well-nigh set, and I can steal away unseen to whisper hope and comfort ere we part forever. Now, Count Rodolpho, thou hast given me another cause for hate. Louis, I can love thee tho' thou art banished and afar.

Hark! 'tis the vesper-bell. Now, courage, heart, and thou shalt mourn no longer.

[*Exit* Leonore.

CURTAIN

SCENE EIGHTH

[*Glen near* Norna's *cave. Enter* Leonore.]

Leonore. Norna is not here, nor Louis. Why comes he not? Surely 'tis the place. Norna! Louis! art thou here?

[*Enter* Rodolpho, *masked.*

Rod. I am here, dear lady. Do not fear me; I may not unmask even to thee, for spies may still be near me. Wilt thou pardon, and still trust me tho' thou canst not see how fondly I am looking on thee. See! here is my ring, my dagger. Oh, Leonore, do not doubt me!

Leonore. I do trust thee; canst thou doubt it now? Oh, Louis! I feared thou wert dead. Why didst thou not tell me all before. And where wilt thou go, and how can I best serve thee? Nought thou canst ask my love shall leave undone.

Rod. Wilt thou let me guide thee to yonder tower? I fear to tell thee here, and old Norna is there waiting for thee. Come, love, for thy Louis's sake, dare yet a little more, and I will tell thee how thou canst serve me. Wilt thou not put thy faith in me, Leonore?

Leonore. I will. Forgive me, if I seem to fear thee; but thy voice sounds strangely hollow, and thine eyes look darkly on me from behind this mask. Thou wilt lay it by when we are safe, and then I shall forget this foolish fear that hangs upon me.

Rod. Thine own hands shall remove it, love. Come, it is not far. Would I might guide thee thus through life! Come, dearest!

[*Exit.*

CURTAIN

SCENE NINTH

[*Castle of* Rodolpho. *The haunted chamber. Enter* Rodolpho *leading* Leonore.]

Leonore. Where art thou leading me, dear Louis? Thy hiding-place is a pleasant one, but where is Norna? I thought she waited for us.

Rod. She will soon be here. Ah, how can I thank thee for this joyful hour, Leonore. I can forget all danger and all sorrow now.

Leonore. Nay, let me cast away this mournful mask! I long to look upon thy face once more. Wilt thou let me, Louis?

Rod. Ay, look upon me if thou wilt;—dost like it, lady? [*Drops his disguise.* Leonore *shrieks, and rushes to the door, but finds it locked.*] 'Tis useless; there are none to answer to thy call. All here are my slaves, and none dare disobey. Where are thy proud words now? hast thou no scornful smile for those white lips, no anger in those beseeching eyes? Where are thy friends? Why come they not to aid thee? Said I not truly my revenge was sure?

Leonore. Oh, pardon me, and pity! See, I will kneel to thee, pray, weep, if thou wilt only let me go. Forgive my careless words! Oh, Count Rodolpho, take me home, and I will forget this cruel jest [*kneels*].

Rod. Ha, ha! It is no jest, and thou hast no home but this. Didst thou not come willingly? I used no force; and all disguise is fair in love. Nay, kneel not to me. Did I not say thou wouldst bend thy proud head, and sue for mercy, and I would deny it? Where is thy defiance now?

Leonore [*rising*]. I'll kneel no more to thee. The first wild fear is past, and thou shalt find me at thy feet no more. As I told thee *then*, I tell thee *now*,—thine I will never be; and think not I will fail or falter at thy threats. Contempt of thee is too strong for fear.

Rod. Not conquered yet. Time will teach thee to speak more courteously to thy master. Ah, thou mayst well look upon these bawbles. They were thy lover's once. This ring was taken from his lifeless hand; this dagger from his bleeding breast, as he lay within

23

the forest whence I led thee. This scroll I found next his heart when it had ceased to beat. I lured thee hither with it, and won my sweet revenge. [Leonore *sinks down weeping.*] Now rest thee; for when the castle clock strikes ten, I shall come to lead thee to the altar. The priest is there,—this ring shall wed thee. Farewell, fair bride; remember,—there is no escape, and thou art mine forever.

Leonore [*starting up*]. Never! I shall be free when thou mayst think help past forever. There is a friend to help me, and an arm to save, when earthly aid is lost. Thine I shall never be! Thou mayst seek me; I shall be gone.

Rod. Thou wilt need thy prayers. I shall return,—remember, when the clock strikes ten, I come to win my bride.

[*Exit.*

Leonore. He has gone, and now a few short hours of life are left to me; for if no other help shall come, death can save me from a fate I loathe. Ah, Louis, Louis, thou art gone forever! Norna, where is thy promise now to guard me? Is there no help? Nor tears nor prayers can melt that cruel heart, and I am in his power. Ha! what is that?— *his* dagger, taken from his dying breast. How gladly would he have drawn it forth to save his poor Leonore! Alas, that hand is cold forever! But I must be calm. He shall see how a weak woman's heart can still defy him, and win liberty by death [*takes the dagger; clock strikes ten*]. It is the hour,—the knell of my young life. Hark! they come. Louis, thy Leonore ere long will join thee, never more to part.

[*The secret panel opens.* Adrian *enters masked.*]

Adrian. Stay, lady! stay thy hand! I come to save thee. Norna sends me,—see, thy token; doubt not, nor delay; another moment, we are lost. Oh, fly, I do beseech thee!

Leonore. Heaven bless thee; I will come. Kind friend, I put a helpless maiden's trust in thee.

Adrian. Stay not! away, away!

[*Exit through the secret panel, which disappears. Enter* Rodolpho.

Rod. Is my fair bride ready? Ha! Leonore, where art thou?

Voice. Gone,—gone forever!

24

Rod. Girl, mock me not; come forth, I say. Thou shalt not escape me. Leonore, answer! Where is my bride?

Voice [*behind the curtains*]. Here—

Rod. Why do I fear? She is there concealed [*lifts the curtain; spirit of* Theresa *rises*]. The fiends! what is that? The spirit haunts me still!

Voice. Forever, forever—

Rod. [*rushes to the door but finds it locked*]. What ho! without there! Beat down the door! Pedro! Carlos! let me come forth! They do not come! Nay, 'tis my fancy; I will forget it all. Still, the door is fast; Leonore is gone. *Who* groans so bitterly? Wild voices are sounding in the air, ghastly faces are looking on me as I turn, unseen hands bar the door, and dead men are groaning in mine ears. I'll not look, not listen; 'tis some spell set on me. Let it pass!

[*Throws himself down and covers his face.*

Voice. The spell will not cease,
The curse will not fly,
And spirits shall haunt
Till the murderer shall die.

Rod. Again, spirit or demon, wherefore dost thou haunt me, and what art thou? [Theresa's *spirit rises.*] Ha! am I gone mad? Unbar the door! Help! help! [*Falls fainting to the floor.*]

[*Enter* Norna.

Norna. Lie there, thou sinful wretch! Old Norna's curse ends but with thy life.

[*Tableau.*

CURTAIN

SCENE TENTH

[*A room in the castle of* Rodolpho. *Enter* Rodolpho.]

Rod. Dangers seem thickening round me. Some secret spy is watching me unseen,—I fear 'tis Hugo, spite the gold I gave him, and the vows he made. A higher bribe may win the secret from him, and then I am undone. Pedro hath told me that a stranger, cloaked and masked, was lurking near the castle on the night when Leonore so strangely vanished [*a laugh*]. Ha!—what's that?—methought I heard that mocking laugh again! I am grown fearful as a child since that most awful night. Well, well, let it pass! If Hugo comes to-night, obedient to the message I have sent, I'll see he goes not hence alive. This cup shalt be thy last, good Hugo! [*Puts poison in the wine-cup.*] He comes,—now for my revenge! [*Enter* Hugo.] Ah, Hugo, welcome! How hath it fared with thee since last we met? Thou lookest weary,—here is wine; sit and refresh thyself.

Hugo. I came not hither, Count Rodolpho, to seek wine, but gold. Hark ye! I am poor; thou art rich, but in my power, for proud and noble though thou art, the low-born Hugo can bring death and dishonor on thy head by whispering one word to the king. Ha!—now give me gold or I will betray thee.

Rod. Thou bold villain, what means this? I paid thee well, and thou didst vow to keep my secret. Threaten me not. Thou art in my power, and shall never leave this room alive. I fear thee not. My menials are at hand,—yield thyself; thou art fairly caught, and cannot now escape me.

Hugo. Nay, not so fast, my lord. One blast upon my horn, and my brave band, concealed below, will answer to my call. Ha! ha! thou art caught, my lord. Thy life is in my hands, and thou must purchase it by fifty good pistoles paid down to me; if not, I will charge thee with the crime thou didst bribe me to perform, and thus win a rich reward. Choose,—thy life is nought to me.

Rod. Do but listen, Hugo. I have no gold; smile if thou wilt, but I am poor. This castle only is mine own, and I am seeking now a rich young bride whose wealth will hide my poverty. Be just, good Hugo,

26

and forgive the harsh words I have spoken. Wait till I am wed, and I will pay thee well.

Hugo. That will I not. I'll have no more of thee, false lord! The king will well reward me, and thou mayst keep thy gold. Farewell! Thou wilt see me once again.

Rod. Stay, Hugo, stay! Give me but time; I may obtain the gold. Wait a little, and it shall be thine. Wilt thou not drink? 'Tis the wine thou likest so well. See! I poured it ready for thee.

Hugo. Nay; I will serve myself. Wine of thy mixing would prove too strong for me [*sits down and drinks*. Rodolpho *paces up and down waiting a chance to stab him*]. Think quickly, my good lord; I must be gone [*turns his head*. R. *raises his dagger*. Hugo *rising*]. I'll wait no more; 'tis growing late, and I care not to meet the spirits which I hear now haunt thy castle. Well, hast thou the gold?

Rod. Not yet; but if thou wilt wait—

Hugo. I tell thee I will not. I'll be deceived no longer. Thou art mine, and I'll repay thy scornful words and sinful deeds by a prisoner's cell. And so, adieu, my lord. Escape is useless, for thou wilt be watched. Hugo is the master now!

[*Exit* Hugo.

Rod. Thou cunning villain, I'll outwit thee yet. I will disguise myself, and watch thee well, and when least thou thinkest it, my dagger shall be at thy breast. And now one thing remains to me, and that is flight. I must leave all and go forth poor, dishonored, and alone; sin on my head, and fear within my heart. Will the sun never set? How slow the hours pass! In the first gloom of night, concealed in yonder old monk's robe, I'll silently glide forth, and fly from Hugo and this haunted house. Courage, Rodolpho, thou shalt yet win a name and fortune for thyself. Now let me rest awhile; I shall need strength for the perils of the night [*lies down and sleeps*].

[*Enter* Norna.

Norna. Poor fool! thy greatest foe is here,—her thou shalt not escape. Hugo shall be warned, and thou alone shalt fall.

[*She makes signs from the window and vanishes.*

Rod. [*awakes and rises*]. Ah, what fearful dreams are mine!

Theresa —Louis—still they haunt me! Whither shall I turn? Who comes? [*Enter* Gaspard.] Art thou another phantom sent to torture me?

Gasp. 'Tis I, leader of the king's brave guards, sent hither to arrest thee, my lord; for thou art charged with murder.

Rod. Who dares to cast so foul a stain on Count Rodolpho's name.

Gasp. My lord, yield thyself. The king may show thee mercy yet—

Rod. I will yield, and prove my innocence, and clear mine honor to the king. Reach me my cloak yonder, and I am ready.

[Gaspard *turns to seek the cloak.* Rodolpho *leaps from the window and disappears.*

Gasp. Ha! he hath escaped,—curses on my carelessness! [*Rushes to the window.*] Ho, there! surround the castle, the prisoner hath fled! We'll have him yet, the blood-stained villain!

[*Exit* Gaspard. *Shouts and clashing of swords heard.*

CURTAIN

SCENE ELEVENTH

[Norna's *cave.* Leonore *and Adrian.*]

Adrian. Dear lady, can I do nought to while away the lonely hours? Shall I go forth and bring thee flowers, or seek thy home and bear away thy bird, thy lute, or aught that may beguile thy solitude? It grieves me that I can do so little for thee.

Leonore. Nay, 'tis I should grieve that I can find no way to show my gratitude to thee, my brave deliverer. But wilt thou not tell me who thou art? I would fain know to whom I owe my life and liberty.

Adrian. Nay, that I may not tell thee. I have sworn a solemn vow, and till that is fulfilled I may not cast aside this sorrowful disguise. Meanwhile, thou mayst call me Adrian. Wilt thou pardon and trust me still?

Leonore. Canst thou doubt my faith in thee? Thou and old Norna are the only friends now left to poor Leonore. I put my whole heart's trust in thee. But if thou canst not tell me of thyself, wilt tell me why thou hast done so much for me, a friendless maiden?

Adrian. I fear it will cause thee sorrow, lady; and thou hast grief enough to bear.

Leonore. Do not fear. I would so gladly know—

Adrian. Forgive me if I make thee weep: I had a friend,—most dear to me. He loved a gentle lady, but ere he could tell her this, he died, and bid me vow to watch above her whom he loved, and guard her with my life. I took the vow: that lady was thyself, that friend Count Louis.

Leonore. Ah, Louis! Louis! that heart thou feared to ask is buried with thee.

Adrian. Thou didst love him, lady?

Leonore. Love him? Most gladly would I lie down within my grave tonight, could I but call him back to life again.

29

Adrian. Grieve not; thou hast one friend who cannot change,—one who through joy and sorrow will find his truest happiness in serving thee. Hist! I hear a step: I will see who comes.

[*Exit* Adrian.

Leonore. Kind, watchful friend, how truly do I trust thee!

[*Re-enter* Adrian.

Adrian. Conceal thyself, dear lady, with all speed. 'Tis Count Rodolpho. Let me lead thee to the inner cave,—there thou wilt be safe.

[*They retire within; noise heard without. Enter* Rodolpho.

Rod. At last I am safe. Old Norna will conceal me till I can find means to leave the land. Ha!—voices within there. Ho, there! old wizard, hither! I have need of thee!

[*Enter* Adrian.

Adrian. What wouldst thou?

Rod. Nought. Get thee hence! I seek old Norna.

Adrian. Thou canst not see her; she is not here.

Rod. Not here? 'Tis false,—I heard a woman's voice within there. Let me pass!

Adrian. 'Tis not old Norna, and thou canst not pass.

Rod. Ah, then, who might it be, my most mysterious sir?

Adrian. The Lady Leonore.

Rod. Ha!—how came she hither? By my soul, thou liest! Stand back and let me go. She is mine!

Adrian. Thou canst only enter here above my lifeless body. Leonore is here, and I am her protector and thy deadliest foe. 'Tis for thee to yield and leave this cell.

Rod. No more of this,—thou hast escaped me once. Draw and defend thyself, if thou hast courage to meet a brave man's sword!

30

Adrian. But for Leonore I would not stoop so low, or stain my sword; but for her sake I'll dare all, and fight thee to the last.

[*They fight their way out. Enter* Rodolpho.

Rod. At length fate smiles upon me. I am the victor,—and now for Leonore! All danger is forgotten in the joy of winning my revenge on this proud girl! Thou art mine at last, Leonore, and mine forever! [*Rushes towards the inner cave. Spirit of* Theresa *rises.*] There 'tis again! I will not fly,—I do defy it! [*Attempts to pass. Spirit touches him; he drops his sword and rushes wildly away.*] 'Tis vain: I cannot—dare not pass. It comes, it follows me. Whither shall I fly?

[*Exit. Enter* Adrian *wounded.*

Adrian. I have saved her once again,—but oh, this deathlike faintness stealing o'er me robs me of my strength. Thou art safe, Leonore, and I am content. [*Falls fainting.*]

[*Enter* Leonore.

 Leonore. They are gone. Ah, what has chanced? I heard his voice, and now 'tis still as death. Where is my friend? God grant he be not hurt! I'll venture forth and seek him [*sees* Adrian *unconscious before her*]. Oh, what is this? Adrian, kind friend, dost thou not hear me? There is blood upon his hand! Can he be dead? No, no! he breathes, he moves; this mask, I will remove it,—surely he will forgive.

[*Attempts to unmask him; he prevents her.*

Adrian [*reviving*]. Nay, nay; it must not be. I am better now. The blow but stunned me,—it will pass away. And thou art safe?

Leonore. I feared not for myself, but thee. Come, rest thee here, thy wound is bleeding; let me bind it with my kerchief, and bring thee wine. Let me serve thee who hath done so much for me. Art better now! Can I do aught else for thee?

Adrian. No more, dear lady. Think not of me, and listen while I tell thee of the dangers that surround thee. Count Rodolpho knows thou art here, and may return with men and arms to force thee hence. My single arm could then avail not, though I would gladly die for thee. Where then can I lead thee,—no place can be too distant, no task too hard for him whose joy it is to serve thee.

31

Leonore. Alas! I know not. I dare not seek my home while Count Rodolpho is my foe; my servants would be bribed,—they would betray me, and thou wouldst not be there to save. Adrian, I have no friend but thee. Oh, pity and protect me!

Adrian. Most gladly will I, dearest lady. Thou canst never know the joy thy confidence hath wakened in my heart. I will save and guard thee with my life. I will guide thee to a peaceful home where no danger can approach, and only friends surround thee. Thy Louis dwelt there once, and safely mayst thou rest till danger shall be past. Will this please thee?

Leonore. Oh, Adrian, thou kind, true friend, how can I tell my gratitude, and where find truer rest than in *his* home, where gentle memories of him will lighten grief. Then take me there, and I will prove my gratitude by woman's fondest friendship, and my life-long trust.

Adrian. Thanks, dear lady. I need no other recompense than the joy 'tis in my power to give thee. I will watch faithfully above thee, and when thou needest me no more, I'll leave thee to the happiness thy gentle heart so well deserves. Now rest, while I seek out old Norna, and prepare all for our flight. The way we have to tread is long and weary. Rest thee, dear lady.

Leonore. Adieu, dear friend. I will await thee ready for our pilgrimage, and think not I shall fail or falter, though the path be long, and dangers gather round us. I shall not fear, for thou wilt be there. God bless thee, Adrian.

[*Tableau.*

CURTAIN

SCENE TWELFTH

[*Room in the castle of* Louis. Leonore *singing to her lute.*]

The weary bird mid stormy skies,
Flies home to her quiet nest,
And 'mid the faithful ones she loves,
Finds shelter and sweet rest.

And thou, my heart, like to tired bird,
Hath found a peaceful home,
Where love's soft sunlight gently falls,
And sorrow cannot come.

Leonore. 'Tis strange that I can sing, but in this peaceful home my sorrow seems to change to deep and quiet joy. Louis seems ever near, and Adrian's silent acts of tenderness beguile my solitary hours, and daily grow more dear to me. He guards me day and night, seeking to meet my slightest wish, and gather round me all I hold most dear. [*Enter a* Page.] Angelo, what wouldst thou?

Page. My master bid me bring these flowers and crave thee to accept them lady.

Leonore. Bear him my thanks, and tell him that his gift is truly welcome. [*Exit* Page.] These are the blossoms he was gathering but now upon the balcony; he hath sent the sweetest and the fairest [*a letter falls from the nosegay*]. But what is here? He hath never sent me aught like this before [*opens and reads the letter*].

Dearest Lady,—Wilt thou pardon the bold words I here address to thee, and forgive me if I grieve one on whom I would bestow only the truest joy. In giving peace to thy heart I have lost mine own. I was thy guide and comforter, and soon, unknown to thee, thy lover. I love thee, Leonore, fondly and truly; and here I ask, wilt thou accept the offering of a heart that will forever cherish thee. If thou canst grant this blessed boon, fling from the casement the white rose I send thee; but if thou canst not accept my love, forgive me for avowing it, and drop the cypress bough I have twined about the rose. I will not pain thee to refuse in words,—the mournful token is enough. Ask thine own heart if thou, who hast loved Louis, can feel aught save friendship for the unknown, nameless stranger, who through life and death is ever

Thy loving Adrian.

Oh, how shall I reply to this,—how blight a love so tender and so true? I have longed to show my gratitude, to prove how I have revered this noble friend. The hour has come when I may make his happiness, and prove my trust. And yet my heart belongs to Louis, and I cannot love another. Adrian was his friend; he loved him, and confided me to him. Nobly hath he fulfilled that trust, and where could I find a truer friend than he who hath saved me from danger and from death, and now gives me the power to gladden and to bless his life. Adrian, if thou wilt accept a sister's love and friendship, they shall be thine. Louis, forgive me if I wrong thee; for though I yield my hand, my heart is thine forever. This rose, Adrian, to thee; this mournful cypress shall be mine in memory of my blighted hopes [*goes to the window and looks out*]. See! he is waiting yonder by the fountain for the token that shall bring him joy or sorrow. Thou noble friend, thy brave, true heart shall grieve no longer, for thus will Leonore repay the debt of gratitude she owes thee [*flings the rose from the window*]. He hath placed it in his bosom, and is coming hither to pour forth his thanks for the poor gift bestowed. I will tell him all, and if he will accept, then I am his.

[*Enter* Adrian *with the rose.*

Adrian. Dear lady, how can I tell thee the joy thou hast given me. This blessed flower from thy dear hand hath told thy pardon and consent. Oh, Leonore, canst thou love a nameless stranger who is so unworthy the great boon thou givest.

Leonore. Listen, Adrian, ere thou dost thank me for a divided heart. Thou hast been told my love for Louis; he was thy friend, and well thou knowest how true and tender was the heart he gave me. He hath gone, and with him rests my first deep love. Thou art my only friend and my protector; thou hast won my gratitude and warmest friendship. I can offer thee a sister's pure affection,—my hand is thine; and here I pledge thee that as thou hast watched o'er me, so now thy happiness shall be my care, thy love my pride and joy. Here is my hand,—wilt thou accept it, Adrian?

Adrian. I will. I would not seek to banish from thy heart the silent

34

love thou bearest Louis. I am content if thou wilt trust me with thy happiness, and give me the sweet right to guide and guard thee through the pilgrimage of life. God bless thee, dearest.

Leonore. Dear Adrian, can I do nought for thee? I have now won the right to cheer thy sorrows. Have faith in thy Leonore.

Adrian. Thou hast a right to know all, and ere long thou shalt. My mysterious vow will now soon be fulfilled, and then no doubt shall part us. Thou hast placed thy trust in me, and I have not betrayed it, and now I ask a greater boon of thy confiding heart. Wilt thou consent to wed me ere I cast aside this mask forever? Believe me, thou wilt not regret it,—'tis part of my vow; one last trial, and I will prove to thee thou didst not trust in vain. Forgive if I have asked too much. Nay, thou canst not grant so strange a boon.

Leonore. I can—I will. I did but pause, for it seemed strange thou couldst not let me look upon thy face. But think not that I fear to grant thy wish. Thy heart is pure and noble, and that thou canst not mask. As I trusted thee through my despair, so now I trust thee in my joy. Canst thou ask more, dear friend?

Adrian. Ever trust me thus! Ah, Leonore, how can I repay thee? My love, my life, are all I can give thee for the blessed gift thou hast bestowed. A time will come when all this mystery shall cease and we shall part no more. Now must I leave thee, dearest. Farewell! Soon will I return.

[*Exit* Adrian.

Leonore. I will strive to be a true and loving wife to thee, dear Adrian; for I have won a faithful friend in thee forever.

CURTAIN

SCENE THIRTEENTH

[*Hall in the castle of* Count Louis. *Enter* Leonore, *in bridal robes.*]

Leonore. At length the hour hath come, when I shall look upon the face of him whom I this day have sworn to love and honor as a wife. I have, perchance, been rash in wedding one I know not, but will not cast a doubt on him who hath proved the noble heart that beats within his breast. I am his, and come what may, the vows I have this day made shall be unbroken. Ah, he comes; and now shall I gaze upon my husband's face!

[*Enter* Adrian.

Adrian. Dearest, fear not. Thou wilt not trust me less when thou hast looked upon the face so long concealed. My vow is ended, thou art won. Thy hand is mine; Leonore, I claim thy heart.

[*Unmasks.* Leonore *screams and falls upon his breast.*

Leonore. Louis, Louis! 'Tis a blessed dream!

Louis. No dream, my Leonore; it is thy living Louis who hath watched above thee, and now claims thee for his own. Ah, dearest, I have tried thee too hardly,—pardon me!

Leonore. Oh, Louis, husband, I have nought to pardon; my life, my liberty, my happiness,—all, all, I owe to thee. How shall I repay thee? [*Weeps upon his bosom.*]

Louis. By banishing these tears, dear love, and smiling on me as you used to do. Here, love, sit beside me while I tell thee my most strange tale, and then no longer shalt thou wonder. Art happy now thy Adrian hath flung by his mask?

Leonore. Happy! What deeper joy can I desire than that of seeing thy dear face once more? But tell me, Louis, how couldst thou dwell so long beside me and not cheer my bitter sorrow when I grieved for thee.

Louis. Ah, Leonore, thou wouldst not reproach me, didst thou know how hard I struggled with my heart, lest I should by some tender word, some fond caress, betray myself when thou didst grieve for me.

36

Leonore. Why didst thou fear to tell thy Leonore? She would have aided and consoled thee. Why didst thou let me pine in sorrow at thy side, when but a word had filled my heart with joy?

Louis. Dearest, I dared not. Thou knowest I was banished by the hate of that fiend Rodolpho. I had a fair and gentle sister, whom he wed, and after cruelty and coldness that I dread to think of now, he murdered her. I sought old Norna's aid. She promised it, and well hath kept her word. When Count Rodolpho's ruffian left me dying in the forest, she saved, and brought me back to life. She bade me take a solemn vow not to betray myself, and to aid her in her vengeance on the murderer of Theresa. Nor could I own my name and rank, lest it should reach the king who had banished me. The vow I took, and have fulfilled.

Leonore. And is there no danger now? Art thou safe, dear Louis, from the Count?

Louis. Fear not, my love. He will never harm us more; his crimes are known. The king hath pardoned me. I have won thee back. He is an outcast, and old Norna's spells have well-nigh driven him mad. My sister, thou art well avenged! Alas! alas! would I could have saved, and led thee hither to this happy home.

Leonore. Ah, grieve not, Louis; she is happy now, and thy Leonore will strive to fill her place. Hast thou told me all?

Louis. Nay, love. Thou knowest how I watched above thee, but thou canst never know the joy thy faithful love for one thou mourned as dead hath brought me. I longed to cast aside the dark disguise I had vowed to wear, but dared not while Rodolpho was at liberty. Now all is safe. I have tried thy love, and found it true. Oh, may I prove most worthy of it, dearest.

Leonore. Louis, how can I love too faithfully the friend who, 'mid his own grief and danger, loved and guarded me. I trusted thee as Adrian; as Louis I shall love thee until death.

Louis. And I shall prize most tenderly the faithful heart that trusted me through doubt and mystery. Now life is bright and beautiful before us, and may you never sorrow that thou gav'st thy heart to Louis, and thy hand to Adrian the "Black Mask."

CURTAIN

37

SCENE FOURTEENTH

[*A dungeon cell.* Rodolpho *chained, asleep. Enter* Norna.]

Norna. Thy fate is sealed, thy course is run,
And Norna's work is well-nigh done.

[*Vanishes. Enter* Hugo.

Rod. [*awaking*]. Mine eyes are bewildered by the forms I have
looked upon in sleep. Methought old Norna stood beside me,
whispering evil spells, calling fearful phantoms to bear me hence.

Hugo [*coming forward*]. Thy evil conscience gives thee little rest,
my lord.

Rod. [*starting up*]. Who is there? Stand back! I'll sell my life most
dearly. Ah, 'tis no dream,—I am fettered! Where is my sword?

Hugo. In my safe keeping, Count Rodolpho, lest in thy rage thou
may'st be tempted to add another murder to thy list of sins.
[Rodolpho *sinks down in despair*.] Didst think thou couldst escape?
Ah, no; although most swift of foot and secret, Hugo hath watched
and followed thee. I swore to win both gold and vengeance. The king
hath offered high reward for thy poor head, and it is mine. Methinks
it may cheer your solitude my lord, so I came hither on my way to
bear thy death warrant to the captain of the guard. What wilt thou
give for this? Hark ye! were this destroyed, thou might'st escape ere
another were prepared. How dost thou like the plot?

Rod. And wilt thou save me, Hugo? Give me not up to the king! I'll
be thy slave. All I possess is thine. I'll give thee countless gold. Ah,
pity, and save me, Hugo!

Hugo. Ha, ha! I did but jest. Thinkest thou I could forego the joy of
seeing thy proud head laid low? Where was thy countless gold when
I did ask it of thee? No, no; thou canst not tempt me to forget my
vengeance. 'Tis Hugo's turn to play the master now. Mayst thou rest
well, and so, good even, my lord.

[*Exit* Hugo.

Rod. Thus end my hopes of freedom. My life is drawing to a close,

38

and all my sins seem rising up before me. The forms of my murdered victims flit before me, and their dying words ring in mine ears,—Leonore praying for mercy at my feet; old Norna whispering curses on my soul. How am I haunted and betrayed! Oh, fool, fool that I have been! My pride, my passion, all end in this! Hated, friendless, and alone, the proud Count Rodolpho dies a felon's death. 'Tis just, 'tis just! [*Enter* Louis *masked*.] What's that? Who spoke? Ah, 'tis mine unknown foe. What wouldst thou here?

Louis. Thou didst bribe one Hugo to murder the young Count Louis, whom thou didst hate. He did thy bidding, and thy victim fell; but Norna saved, and healed his wounds. She told him of his murdered sister's fate, and he hath joined her in her work of vengeance, and foiled thee in thy sinful plots. I saved Leonore, and guarded her till I had won her heart and hand, and in her love find solace for the sorrow thou hast caused. Dost doubt the tale? Look on thine unknown foe, and find it true [*unmasks*].

Rod. Louis, whom I hated, and would kill,—thou here, thou husband of Leonore, happy and beloved! It is too much, too much! If thou lovest life, depart. I'm going mad: I see wild phantoms whirling round me, voices whispering fearful words within mine ears. Touch me not,—there is blood upon my hands! Will this dream last forever?

Louis. May Heaven pity thee! Theresa, thou art avenged.

[*Exit* Louis.

Rod. Ah, these are fearful memories for a dying hour! [*Casts himself upon the floor.*]

[*Enter* Norna.

Norna. Sinful man, didst think thy death-bed could be peaceful? As they have haunted thee in life, so shall spirits darken thy last hour. *I* bore thy murdered wife to a quiet grave, and raised a spirit to affright and haunt thee to thy death. *I* freed the Lady Leonore; *I* mocked and haunted thee in palace, wood, and cell; *I* warned Hugo, and betrayed thee to his power; and *I* brought down this awful doom upon thee. As thou didst refuse all mercy to thy victims, so shall mercy be denied to thee. Remorse and dark despair shall wring thy heart, and thou shalt die unblessed, unpitied, unforgiven. Thy victims are avenged, and Norna's work is done.

[Norna *vanishes*.

Rod. Ha! ha! 'tis gone,—yet stay, 'tis Louis' ghost! How darkly his eyes shine on me! See, see,—the demons gather round me! How fast they come! Old Norna is there, muttering her spells. Let me go free! Unbind these chains! Hugo, Louis, Leonore, Theresa,—thou art avenged!

[*Falls dead.* Norna *glides in and stands beside him.*

[*Tableau.*

CURTAIN

CAPTIVE OF CASTILE;

OR,

THE MOORISH MAIDEN'S VOW

CHARACTERS

Bernardo *Lord of Castile*.

Ernest L'Estrange *An English Lord*.

Hernando *A Priest*.

Selim *A Slave*.

Zara *Daughter to Bernardo*.

SCENE FIRST

[*A thick wood. Storm coming on. Enter* Ernest.]

Ernest. This summer sky, darkened by storm, is a fit emblem of my life. O happy England, why did I leave thee; why let dreams of fame and honor win me from a home, to wander now a lonely and bewildered fugitive? But why do I repine? Life, health, and a brave heart yet are mine; and 'mid all my peril, God may send some joy to cheer me on to happiness and honor. Hist! a footstep. 'Tis a light one, but a Moorish foe steals like a serpent on his prey. I'll hide me here, and if need be I'll sell my life as a brave man should [*conceals himself among the trees*].

[*Enter* Zara, *weeping.*

Zara. Heaven shield me! Whither shall I turn? Alone in this wild forest, where may I find a friend to help. The dark storm gathers fast, and I am shelterless. The fierce Spaniard may be wandering nigh, and I dare not call for aid. Mistress of a hundred slaves, here must I perish for one to lead me. Father, the faint heart turns to thee when earthly help is past; hear and succor thy poor child now, who puts her trust in thee.

Ernest [*coming forward*]. Lady, thy prayer is heard. God hath not sent me here in vain. How may I best serve thee?

Zara. Gentle stranger, pity and protect a hapless maid who puts her faith in thee. Guide me from this wild wood, and all the thanks a grateful heart can give are thine.

Ernest. I ask no higher honor than to shield so fair a flower from the storm, or from rude hands that may harm it. But how chanced it, lady, that thou art wandering thus unattended? 'Tis unsafe for youth and beauty while the Spanish army is so near.

Zara. It was a foolish fancy led me hither, and dearly am I punished. Journeying from a distant convent to my father's home, while my attendants rested by a spring I wandered through the wood, unthinking of the danger, till turning to retrace my steps, I found myself lost and alone. I feared to call, and but for thee, kind

42

stranger, might have never seen my home again. Ask not my name, but tell me thine, that in my prayers I may remember one who has so aided me.

Ernest. It were uncourteous to refuse thy bidding, lady. Ernest L'Estrange is the name now honored by the poor service I may do thee. In the Spanish army I came hither, and fear I have seen the last of home or friends. The Moors now seek my life, and ere I can rejoin my ranks, I may be a slave. But the storm draws nearer. Let me lead thee to some shelter, lady.

Zara. Methinks I see a glimmer yonder. Let us seek it, for with thee I fear no longer. I can only give thee thanks, most noble stranger; yet a day may come when she for whom thou dost now risk thy life may find a fit return, worthy thy courtesy to one so helpless and forlorn.

[*Exit* Ernest *and* Zara.

CURTAIN

SCENE SECOND

[*Room in the castle of* Bernardo. Zara *alone*].

Zara. 'Tis strange how the thought haunts me still. Long months have passed since last I saw that noble face, and yet those gentle eyes look on me! Ernest!—'tis a sweet English name, and 'twas a noble English heart that felt such tender pity for a helpless maid. Hark! my father's step! He comes to tell of victories gained, of kingdoms won. Oh, would he might bring some word of him I have so longed to see and thank once more!

[*Enter* Bernardo *with a casket.*

Ber. Joyful tidings, Zara! Grenada is free. Here, love, are gems for thee; they have shone on many a fair lady's neck, but none more fair than thine. And here are things more precious far to me than all their gold and gems,—a goodly list of prisoners taken in the fight, and sent to cool their Spanish blood in our deepest cells. Ah, many a proud name is here,—Ferdinand Navarre, Carlos of Arragon, Lord L'Estrange, and Baron Lisle. But, child, what ails thee?

Zara [*starting up*]. L'Estrange! Is he a prisoner too? Hast thou read aright? Father, Father, it was he who saved me from a bitter death in yonder forest. I never told his name lest it should anger thee. For my sake spare him, and let the gratitude thou hast felt for that kind deed soften thy heart to the brave stranger.

Ber. Nay, Zara! He is thy country's foe, and must be sacrificed to save her honor. 'Twas a simple deed thou hast spoken of. What brave man but would save a fair girl from storms or danger? 'Tis a foolish thought, love; let it pass.

Zara. Oh, Father! I who never bent the knee to man before, implore thee thus [*kneels*]. Be merciful! Leave not the English lord to the dark and fearful doom that waits him. I know too well the life-long captivity, more terrible than death itself, that is his fate. Oh, speak! Say he is forgiven, Father!

Ber. Nay, what wild dream is this? Listen, child! I tell thee he must suffer the captivity he merits as thy country's foe. He hath borne arms against thy king, slain thy kindred, brought woe and desolation thro' the land our fathers gave us. And thou wouldst

44

plead for him! Shame on thee! Thou art no true daughter of thy suffering country if thou canst waste one tear on those who were well lodged in our most dreary dungeons. Call thy pride to aid thee, Zara, and be worthy of thy noble name.

Zara. Father, thou hast often told me woman's lot was 'mid the quiet scenes of home, and that no thoughts of fame or glory should lie within a heart where only gentleness and love should dwell; but I have learned to honor bravery and noble deeds, and I would pledge my troth for the noble stranger. See the English knight, and if he win thee not to gratitude, thou art not the tender father who, through long years, hath so loved and cherished thy motherless child.

Ber. Nay, Zara, nay; honor is a sterner master than a father's love. I cannot free the captive till the king who hath sealed his doom shall pardon also. The prisoners are men of rank, and for thy country's sake must die. Forget thy foolish fancy, child, and set thy young heart on some fairer toys than these false English lords. Adieu, love; I must to the council.

[*Exit* Bernardo.

Zara. Ah, there was a time when Zara's lightest wish was gladly granted. This cruel war hath sadly changed my father; he hath forgotten all his generous pity for suffering and sorrow. But my work is yet undone, and the stranger is a captive. He *shall* be free, and I will pay the debt of gratitude I owe him. I will brave my father's anger; but whom can I trust to aid me? Ha! Selim! He is old and faithful, and will obey [*claps her hands*].

[*Enter* Selim.

Selim. Your bidding, lady.

Zara. Selim, thou hast known me from my birth, and served me well. I have done thee many a kindness. Wilt thou grant me one that shalt repay all that I have ever shown to thee?

Selim. Lady, thou hast made a slave's life happy by thy care, and through the long years I have served thee, hast never bid me do aught that was not right. If my poor services can aid thee now, they are most gladly thine.

Zara. Listen, Selim, while I tell thee what I seek. Thou knowest an English soldier saved and led me from the forest yonder, and thou knowest how my father thanked and blessed the unknown friend who had so aided me. Yet now, when it is in his power to show the gratitude he felt, he will not, and has doomed the man he once longed to honor to a lonely cell to pine away a brave heart's life in sorrow and captivity. I would show that gentle stranger that a woman never can forget. I would free him. Thou hast the keys. This is the service I now crave of thee.

Selim. Lady, canst thou ask me to betray the trust my lord, thy father, hath been pleased to place in me? Ask anything but this, and gladly will I obey thee.

Zara. Ah, must I ever ask and be refused? Selim, listen! Thou hast a daughter; she is fair and young, and thou hast often sighed that she should be a slave. If thou wilt aid me now, the hour the chains fall from the English captive's limbs, that hour shalt see thy daughter free, and never more a slave. If thou wilt win this joy for her, then grant my prayer, and she is free.

Selim. Oh, lady, lady, tempt me not! much as I love my child, I love mine honor more. I cannot aid thee to deceive thy father.

Zara. Nay, Selim, I do not ask it of thee. The proud name my father bears shall ne'er be stained by one false deed of mine. I ask thee but to lead me to the prisoner's cell, that I may offer freedom, and tell him woman's gratitude can never fail, nor woman's heart forget. And if my father ask thee aught of this, thou shalt answer freely. Tell him all, and trust his kindness to forgive; and if evil come *I* will bear it bravely,—thou shalt not suffer. Thou shalt win thy fair child's freedom, and my fadeless thanks.

Selim. Thou hast conquered, lady; and for the blessed gift that is my reward, I will brave all but treachery and dishonor. Thou shalt find thy truest slaves in the old man and his daughter [*kneels and gives the keys*].

Zara. Thanks, good Selim, thanks; thou shalt find a grateful friend in her thou hast served so well. I will disguise me as a female slave, and thou shalt lead me to the cell. Now go; I will join thee anon. [*Exit* Selim.] Oh, Ernest, Ernest! Thy brave heart shall pine no longer. Another hour, and thou art free. Chains cannot bind, nor dungeons hold when woman's love and gratitude are thine.

[*Exit.*

CURTAIN

SCENE THIRD

[*Dungeon in the castle of* Bernardo. Ernest L'Estrange, *chained.*]

Ernest. So end my dreams of fame and honor! A life-long captive, or a sultan's slave are all that fate has left me now. Yet, 'mid disgrace and sorrow, one thought can cheer me yet, and one sweet vision brighten e'en my dreary lot. I have served my country well, and won the thanks of Spain's most lovely daughter. Sweet lady, little does she dream amid her happiness that memories of her are all now left to cheer a captive's heart. But hist!—a footstep on the stair. Perchance they come to lead me forth to new captivity or death. [*Enter* Zara, *disguised as a slave*] Ah, who comes here to cheer the cell of the poor captive?

Zara. Captive no longer, if life and liberty be dear to thee. Say but the word, and ere the sun sets thou shalt be free amid the hills of Spain.

Ernest. Who art thou, coming like a spirit to my lonely cell, bringing hopes of freedom? Tell me, what hath moved thee to such pity for an unknown stranger?

Zara. Not unknown to her I serve. She hath not forgot thee, noble stranger. When thou didst lead her from the dim wood, she said a day might come when she, so weak and helpless then, might find some fit reward for one who risked his life for her. That hour hath come, and she hath sent her poor slave hither, and with her thanks and blessing to speed thee on thy way.

Ernest. And is she near, and did she send thee to repay my simple deed with one like this? Ah, tell her name! Where doth she dwell, and whence the power to set me free?

Zara. I may not tell thee more than this. Her father is Bernardo of Castile. She heard thy name among the captives doomed, and seeks to save thee; for if thou dost not fly, a most cruel death awaits thee. Listen to her prayer, and cast these chains away.

Ernest. It cannot be. Much as I love my freedom, I love my honor more; and I am bound until my conqueror shall give back my plighted word, to seek no freedom till he shall bid me go. Nay, do not sigh, kind friend; I am no longer sad. From this day forth captivity is sweet. Tell thy fair mistress all my thanks are hers; but I may not take the gift she offers, for with freedom comes dishonor, and I cannot break my word to her stern father. Tell her she hath made my fetters light, this cell a happy home, by the sweet thought that she is near and still remembers one who looks upon the hour when first we met as the happiest he hath known.

Zara. If there be power in woman's gratitude, thou shalt yet be free, and with thine honor yet unstained. She will not rest till all the debt she owes thee is repaid. Farewell, and think not Zara will forget [*turns to go; her veil falls*].

Ernest [*starting*]. Lady!—and is it thou? Ah, leave me not! Let me thank thee for the generous kindness which has made a lone heart happy by the thought that even in this wild land there is still one to remember the poor stranger.

Zara. Pardon what may seem to thee unmaidenly and bold; but thou wert in danger; there were none whom I could trust. Gratitude hath bid me come, and I am here. Again I ask, nay, I implore thee, let me have the joy of giving freedom to one brave English heart. England is thy home: wouldst thou not tread its green shores once again? Are there no fond hearts awaiting thy return? Ah, can I not tempt thee by all that man most loves, to fly?

Ernest. Lady, my own heart pleads more earnestly than even thy sweet voice; but those kind eyes were better dimmed with tears for my sad death than be turned coldly from me as one who had stained the high name he bore. And liberty were dearly purchased if I left mine honor here behind. Ask me no more; for till thy father sets me free, I am his prisoner here. Ah, dearest lady, thou hast made this lone cell bright, and other chains than these now hold me here.

Zara. Then it must be. Much as I grieve for thy captivity, I shall honor thee the more for thy unfailing truth, more prized than freedom, home, or friends. And though I cannot save thee now, thou shalt find a Moorish maiden true and fearless as thyself. Farewell! May happy thoughts of home cheer this dark cell till I have won the power to set thee free.

[*Exit* Zara.

48

Ernest. Liberty hath lost its charms since thou art near me, lovely Zara. These chains are nothing now, for the fetters that thy beauty, tenderness, and grace have cast about my heart are stronger far.

CURTAIN

SCENE FOURTH

[Zara's *chamber. Enter* Bernardo.]

Ber. [*unfolding a scroll*]. At length 't is done, and here I hold the doom of those proud lords who have so scorned my race. The hour has come, and Bernardo is revenged. What, ho! Zara, where art thou?

[*Enter* Zara.

Zara. Dear father, what hath troubled thee, and how can Zara cheer and comfort thee?

Ber. 'Tis joy, not sorrow, Zara, gives this fierce light to mine eye. I have hated, and am avenged. This one frail scroll is dearer far to me than all the wealth of Spain, for 'tis the death-knell of the English lords.

Zara. Must they all die, my father?

Ber. Ay, Zara,—all; ere to-morrow's sun shall set they will sleep forever, and a good deed will be well done. I hate them, and their paltry lives can ill repay the sorrow they have wrought.

Zara. Let me see the fatal paper. [*Takes the scroll; aside.*] Yes, *his* name is here. Ah, how strange that these few lines can doom brave hearts to such a death! [*Aloud.*] Father, 'tis a fearful thing to hold such power over human life. Ah, bid me tear the scroll, and win for thee the thanks of those thy generous pity saves.

Ber. [*seizing the paper*]. Not for thy life, child! Revenge is sweet, and I have waited long for mine. The king hath granted this; were it destroyed, the captives might escape ere I could win another. Nay, Zara, this is dearer to me than thy most priceless gems. To-night it shall be well guarded 'neath my pillow. Go to thy flowers, child. These things are not for thee,—thou art growing pale and sad. Remember, Zara, thou art nobly born, and let no foolish pity win thee to forget it.

[*Exit* Bernardo.

50

Zara. Oh, Father, Father, whom I have so loved and honored, now so cold, so pitiless. The spirit of revenge hath entered thy kind heart, and spread an evil blight o'er all the flowers that blossomed there. I cannot win him back to tenderness, and Ernest, thou must perish. I cannot save thee,—perhaps 'tis better so; but oh, 'twill be a bitter parting! [*Weeps.*] Nay, nay, it shall *not* be! When this wild hate hath passed, my father will repent. Alas! 't will be too late. *I* will save him from that sorrow when he shall find he hath wronged a noble heart, and slain the friend he should have saved. But stay! how shall I best weave my plot? That fatal paper, once destroyed, I will implore and plead so tenderly, my father will repent; and ere another scroll can reach his hands, I will have won thy freedom, Ernest! This night beneath his pillow it will be; and I, like a midnight thief, must steal to that couch, and take it hence. Yet, it shall be done, for it will save thee, Father, from a cruel deed, and gain a brave heart's freedom. Ernest, 'tis for thee! for thee!

CURTAIN

SCENE FIFTH

[*Chamber in the castle*. Bernardo *sleeping*. *Enter* Zara.]

Zara. He sleeps calmly as a child. Why do I tremble? 'T is a deed of mercy I would do, and thou wilt thank me that I dared to disobey, and spare thee from life-long regret. The paper,—yes, 'tis here! Forgive me, Father; 'tis to save thee from an evil deed thy child comes stealing thus at dead of night to take what thou hast toiled so long to win. Sleep on! no dark dream can break thy slumber now; the spirit of revenge shall pass away, and I will win thee back to pity and to love once more. Now, Ernest, thou art saved, and ere to-morrow's sun shall rise this warrant for thy death shall be but ashes, and my task be done.

[*Exit* Zara.

CURTAIN

SCENE SIXTH

[Zara's *chamber*. Zara *alone*].

Zara. The long, sleepless night at length hath passed. The paper is destroyed, and now nought remains but to confess the deed, and brave my father's anger.

[*Enter* Bernardo.

Ber. Zara!

Zara [*starts*]. Why so stern, my father? Hath thy poor Zara angered thee?

Ber. I have trusted thee as few would trust a child. Thou art fair and gentle, and I had thought true. Never, Zara, till now hast thou deceived me; and if thou wouldst keep thy father's love and trust, I bid thee answer truly. Didst thou, in the dead of night steal to my pillow, and bear hence the paper I had told thee would be there? Thy slave girl, Zillah, missed thee from thy couch, and saw thee enter there. She feared to follow, but none other came within my chamber, and this morn the scroll is gone. Now answer, Zara! Didst thou take the warrant, and where is it now?

Zara. Burnt to ashes, and scattered to the winds. I have never stained my soul with falsehood, and I will not now. Oh, Father! I have loved and honored thee through the long years thou hast watched above me. How could I love on when thou hadst stained with blood that hand that blessed me when a child, how honor when thou hadst repaid noble deeds with death? Forgive me that I plead for those thou hast doomed! I alone am guilty,—let thine anger fall on me; but, Father, I implore thee, leave this evil deed undone. [*Kneels*.]

Ber. Thou canst plead well for thy father's and thy country's foe. What strange fancy hath possessed thee, Zara? Thou hast never wept, tho' many a Christian knight hath pined and died within these walls; and even now, methinks, thou speakest more of gratitude than mercy, and seem strangely earnest for the English lord who did thee some small service long ago. Speak, Zara! wouldst thou save

53

them *all*? Were I to grant thee all their lives save his, wouldst thou be content to let *him* die?

Zara. Nay, Father; but for his tender care thou wouldst have no daughter now to stand before thee, pleading for the life he bravely risked in saving mine. Oh, would I had died amid the forest leaves ere I had brought such woe to him, and lived to lose my father's love! [*Weeps.*]

Ber. Listen, Zara! Little as I know of woman's heart, I have learned to read thine own; and if I err not, thou hast dared to love this stranger. Ha! is it so? Girl, I command thee to forget that love, and leave him to his fate!

Zara. Never! I will not forget the love that like a bright star hath come to cheer my lonely heart. I will *not* forget the noble friend who, 'mid his fiercest foes, could brave all dangers to restore an unknown maiden to her home. And when I offered liberty (for I have disobeyed and dared to seek his cell), he would not break the word he had plighted, Father, unto thee. He bade me tempt him not, for death were better than dishonor. Ah, canst thou doom him to a felon's death? Then do it; and the hour that sees that true heart cease to beat, that hour thou hast lost the child who would have loved and clung to thee through life.

Ber. Child, thou hast moved me strangely. I would grant thy prayer, but thou shalt never wed one of that accursed race. I bear no hate to the young lord, save that he is thy country's foe; and if he gains his freedom, he will win thee too. By Allah! it shall never be. Yet, listen, Zara! If I grant his life wilt thou ask no more?

Zara. 'T is all I ask; grant me but this, and I will give thee all the gratitude and love this poor heart can bestow.

Ber. Then 'tis done. Yet hold! the price that thou must pay for this dear boon is large. Thou must swear never to see him more; must banish love, nay, even memory of that fatal hour when first he saw and saved thee. If thou wilt vow to wed none but one of thine own race, his life and liberty are thine to give. Speak, Zara! Wilt thou do all this?

Zara. Oh, Father, Father, anything but this! Pity, gratitude, and love have bound me to him, and the fetters thou hast cast around him are not stronger than the deep affection he hath wakened in my

54

heart. Ah, why wilt thou not give life and liberty to him, and joy to thy child? I will not take the vow.

Ber. Then his fate is sealed. Thy girl's heart is too selfish to forego its own joy for his sake. Thou dost not love enough to sacrifice thy happiness to win his freedom. I had thought more nobly of thee, Zara.

Zara. I *will* be worthy all thou mayst have thought me; but thou canst little know the desolation thou hast brought me. Thou shalt see how deeply thou hast wronged me, and my love. I will bear all, suffer all, if it will win the life and liberty of him I love so deeply and so well.

Ber. Would to Heaven thou hadst never seen this English stranger! Again, and for the last time, Zara, I ask thee, Wilt thou leave the captive to his fate, and seek another heart to love?

Zara. Never! I could mourn his death with bitter tears; but oh, my love is worthy a deeper sacrifice! He shall never suffer one sad hour if I may spare him, and never know that liberty to him will bring such life-long sorrow unto me.

Ber. Then thou wilt take the vow I bid thee?

Zara. I will.

Ber. Then swear by all thou dost hold most dear, and by thy mother's spirit, to wed one only of thy father's race; and through joy and sorrow, thro' youth and age, to keep thy vow unbroken until death.

Zara. I swear; and may the spirit of that mother look in pity on the child whose love hath made her life so dark a path to tread.

Ber. May thou find comfort, Zara! I would have spared thee this, but now it cannot be. Yet thy reward shall well repay thee for thy sacrifice. The English knight is free, and thou shalt restore him unto life and liberty. May Allah bless thee, child!

[*Exit* Bernardo.

Zara. 'Tis over! The bright dream is past. Oh, Ernest! few will love thee as I have done; few suffer for thee all that I so gladly bear; and none can honor thy true, noble heart more tenderly than she whose hard lot it is to part from thee forever. Still amid my blighted hopes one thought can brighten my deep sorrow,—this sacrifice but renders me more worthy of thee, Ernest. Now farewell, love; my poor heart may grieve for its lost joy, and look for comfort but in Heaven.

CURTAIN

SCENE SEVENTH

[*The cell.* Ernest *chained. Enter* Zara.]

Zara. My lord, I seek thee with glad tidings.

Ernest. Why so pale, dear lady? Let no care for me dim thine eye, or chase the roses from thy cheek. I would not barter this dark cell while thou art here for a monarch's fairest home.

Zara. Thou wilt gladly leave it when I tell thee thy captivity is o'er, and I am here to set thee free. I have won thy liberty, and thou mayst fly with honor all unstained; for here my father grants thy pardon, and now bids thee go.

Ernest. How can I thank thee for thy tenderness and pity; how may I best show the gratitude I owe thee for the priceless boon of freedom thou hast this day given?

Zara. Nay, spare thy thanks! I have but paid the debt I owed thee, and 'tis but life for life. Now haste; for ere the sunset hour thou must be beyond the city gates, and on thy way to home and happiness [*takes off his chains*]. And now, brave heart, thou art free, and Zara's task is done [*turns to go*].

Ernest. Stay, lady! thou hast loosed the chains that bound these hands, but oh, thou hast cast a stronger one around my heart; and with my liberty comes love, and thoughts of thee, thy beauty, tenderness, and all thou hast done for me. Lady, thou hast cast away my fetters, but I am captive still [*he kneels*]. Ah, listen, Zara, while I tell thee of the love that like a sweet flower hath blossomed in this dreary cell, and made e'en liberty less precious than one word, one smile from thee.

Zara. I may not listen,—'tis too late, and 'tis a sin for me to hear thee. Ah, ask me not why, but hasten hence, and leave me to the fate thou canst not lighten.

Ernest. Never! I will not leave thee till I have won the right to cheer and comfort her who has watched so fearlessly o'er me. Tell me all, and let me share thy sorrow, Zara.

57

Zara. Ah, no! It cannot be! Thou canst not break my solemn vow. Go! leave me! Heaven bless thee, and farewell!

Ernest. A solemn vow! Hast thou bound thyself to win my freedom? Then never will I leave this cell till thou hast told me all. I swear it, and I will keep the oath.

Zara. Ernest, I implore thee, fly, or it may be too late. Thou canst not help me, and I will not tell thee. Ah, leave me! I cannot save thee if thou tarry now.

Ernest. Never, till thou hast told me by what noble sacrifice thou hast saved this worthless life of mine. Let me free thee from thy sorrow, Zara, or help thee bear it. Thou hast won my pardon, and I will not go till thou hast told me how.

Zara. And wilt thou promise to go hence when I have told thee all, and let me have the joy of knowing thou art safe?

Ernest. I *will* leave thee, Zara, if thou canst bid me go. Now tell me all thy sorrow, love, and let me share it with thee.

Zara. Ernest, I sought to save thee; for I had learned to love the noble stranger who had done so kind a deed for me. I sought to win my father back to gratitude. I wept and sued in vain,—he would not grant thy life, the boon for which I prayed. Alone I watched above thee, and when the warrant for thy death was sent, I took it from his pillow and destroyed it. Thou wast safe. My father charged me with the deed; and when I told him all, he bid me love no more, and leave thee to thy fate. He bid me show how strong my woman's heart could be, and told me if I yet desired thy freedom, I might win it if I took a solemn vow to wed none but of my father's race. I took the vow, and thou art free. Ah, no more!—and let us part while yet I have the strength to say farewell.

Ernest. And is it yet too late? Canst thou not take back the vow, and yet be mine? I cannot leave thee,—rather be a captive here till thou shalt set me free. Come, Zara, fly with me, and leave the father who would blight thy life to satisfy a fierce revenge. Ah, come and let me win thee back to love and happiness.

Zara. Ernest, tempt me not. By that sad vow I swore by all my future hopes, and by my dead mother's spirit, I would never listen to thy words of love. And stern and cruel tho' my father be, I cannot leave him now. Deep and bitter though this sorrow be, 'tis nobler far to

58

bear the burden than to cast it down and seek in idle joys to banish penitence; for thorns would lie amid the flowers. Farewell! Forget me, and in happy England find some other heart to gladden with thy love. Oh, may she prove as fond and faithful as thy Moorish Zara.

Ernest. I will plead no more, nor add to that sad heart another sorrow. I will be worthy such true love, and though we meet no more on earth, in all my wanderings sweet tender thoughts of thee shall dwell within my heart. I will bear my sorrow as a brave man should. The life thou hast saved and brightened by thy love shall yet be worthy thee. Farewell! May all the blessings a devoted heart can give rest on thee, dearest. Heaven bless thee, and grant that we shall meet again.

[*Exit.*

Zara. Gone, gone, forever! Oh, Father, couldst thou know the deep grief and despair thy cruelty has brought two loving hearts, thou wouldst relent, and call them back to happiness. Where can I look for comfort now? [*Weeps.*] I will seek the good priest who hath so long watched above the motherless child. I must find rest in some kind heart, and he will cheer, and teach me how to suffer silently. I will seek old Hernando's cell.

[*Exit* Zara.

CURTAIN

SCENE EIGHTH

[*Cell of the priest.* Hernando *reading. Enter* Zara.]

Zara. Father, I have come for help and counsel. Wilt thou give it now as thou hast ever done to her who comes to learn of thee how best to bear a sorrow cheerfully and well?

Her. Speak on, dear child. I know thy sorrow. Thou hast loved, and sacrificed thy own life's joy to win a brave heart's freedom. Thou hast done nobly and well; thy sorrow will but render thee more worthy of the happiness thou hast so truly won.

Zara. No, no; we shall never meet again on earth. Ah, holy father, they who told thee of my love for one who well might win the noblest heart, have told thee but the lightest part of the deep grief that bears me down. Listen to me, Father, and then give me comfort if thou canst. To win my lover's freedom, I have sworn a solemn oath to wed none but of my father's race. Ernest came from sunny England, and I am the daughter of a Moorish lord. Alas, 'tis vain to hope! The vow is given, and must be kept.

Her. Ay, Zara, and it may be kept; but these sad tears will change to sighs of joy when I have told thee all. Then thou wilt bless the vow which brings thee sorrow now.

Zara. Oh, speak! Tell me what joy canst thou give to lighten grief like mine! Give me not too much hope; for if it fail, despair thou canst not banish will cast a deeper gloom o'er this poor heart. Now, tell me all.

Her. Calm thyself, poor child; it will be well with thee, and thou shalt yet blossom in thy loveliness beside the heart thou hast won. I will tell thee the true tale of thy fair mother's life. She loved and wed a stranger, and thus won the hatred of her Moorish kindred, who sought to win her for their prince's bride. And when she fled away with him to whom her true heart's love was given, they vowed a fierce revenge. Years passed away; she drooped and died. Thy father perished bravely on the field of battle, and left his child to me. I stood beside thy mother's dying bed, and vowed to guard her babe till thou wert safe among thy Moorish kindred. I have watched thee

60

well, and thou art worthy all the happiness thy true heart hath won. Bernardo of Castile is but thy mother's friend; thy father was an English lord, and thou canst keep thy vow, and yet wed the brave young Englishman who hath won thy love.

Zara. Heaven pardon this wild, wilful heart that should mourn the sorrow sent, when such deep joy as this is given. Ah, Father, how can I best thank thee for the blessed comfort thou hast given?

Her. Thy joy, dear child, is my reward. When thou art safe with him thou lovest, my task on earth is done, and I shall pass away with happy thoughts of the sweet flower that bloomed beside the old man's path through life, and cheered it with her love. Bless thee, my Zara, and may the spirit of thy mother watch above thee in the happy home thou hast gained by thy noble sacrifice.

Zara. Oh, Father, may the joy thy words have brought me brighten thine own life as they have mine. The blessings of a happy heart be on thee. Farewell, Father!

[*Kneels, kisses his hand. Exit.*

CURTAIN

SCENE NINTH

[*Hall in the castle. Enter* Zara.]

Zara. Selim said the packet would be here [*takes the paper*]. Ah, 'tis from Ernest! He is near me,—we may meet again [*opens letter and reads*].

> Lady,—Thy father will this night betray the city to the Spanish king, who hath promised his life and liberty for this treachery. He will not keep his oath, and thy father will be slain. Then bid him fly, and save all he most loves, for no mercy will be shown to those within the walls when once the Spanish army enters there. Save thyself. Heaven bless thee.
>
> Ernest.

Brave and true unto the last! O heart! thou mayst well beat proudly, for thou hast won a noble prize in the love of Ernest L'Estrange. Time flies; this night the city is betrayed, and we must fly. Bernardo, lord of fair Castile, is a traitor. Ah, thank Heaven he is *not* my father! Yet for the love I bore him as a child, he shall be saved; and I will cheer and comfort him now that the dark hour of his life has come.

[*Enter* Bernardo.

Ber. Zara, why dost thou look thus on me? I come to bid thee gather all thou dost most prize, for the army is before the city, and we may be conquered ere to-morrow's sun shall set.

Zara. Seek not to deceive me. I know all; and the love I bore thee as my father is now turned to pity and contempt for the traitor who will this night betray Castile.

Ber. Girl, beware, lest thy wild folly anger me too far! What meanest thou? Who has dared to tell thee this?

Zara. Thou wouldst betray, and art thyself betrayed; and were it not for him whom thou hast wronged and hunted, ere to-morrow's dawn thou wouldst be no more, and I a homeless wanderer. Here! read the scroll, and see how well the false king keeps his word he plighted thee for thy deed of treachery.

Ber. [*reads, and drops the paper*]. Lost! lost! Fool that I was to trust the promise of a king! Disgraced, dishonored, and betrayed! Where find a friend to help me now? [*Weeps.*]

Zara. Here,—in the child who clings to thee through danger, treachery, and death. Trust to the love of one whom once thou loved, and who still longs to win thee back to happiness and honor.

Ber. Nay, child, I trust thee not. I have deceived thee and blighted all thy hopes of love. Thou canst not care for the dishonored traitor. Go! tell my guilt to those I would this night deliver up to death, and win a deep revenge for all the wrong I have done thee. I am in thy power now.

Zara [*tearing the paper*]. And thus do I use it! No eye shall ever read these words that do betray thee; no tongue call down dishonor on thy head. Thy plot is not yet known, and ere to-night the gates may be well guarded. Thou mayst fly in safety, and none ever know the stain upon thy name. Thou whom I once called father, this is my revenge. I know all the wrong thou hast done me,—the false vow I made to save the life of him I loved. Zara's pity and forgiveness are thine, freely given; and her prayer is that thou mayst find happiness in some fair land where only gentle thoughts and loving memories may be thine.

Ber. Thou hast conquered, Zara; my proud heart is won by thy tender pity and most generous pardon to one who hath so deeply wronged thee. But I will repay the debt I owe thee. Thou shalt find again the loving father and the faithful friend of thy young life. Thou shalt know how well Bernardo can atone for all the sorrow he hath brought thee.

Zara. And I will be again thy faithful child.

Ber. 'Tis well; and now, my Zara, ere the dawn of another day we must be far beyond the city gates. Selim shall guide us, and once free, together we will seek another and a happier home. Courage, my child, and haste thee. I will prepare all for our flight. Remember, when the turret bell strikes seven, we meet again.

[*Embraces* Zara, *and exit.*

Zara. Farewell! I will not fail thee. Love, joy, and hope may fade, but duty still remains. Oh, Ernest, couldst thou but see thy own true Zara now! Wouldst thou could aid me! [*Enter* Ernest *disguised.*] Ah, who comes? A stranger. Speak! thine errand!

Ernest [*kneeling, presents a scroll*]. An English knight without the gates did bid me seek thee with this scroll. May it please thee, read.

Zara [*opens and reads*].

> Lady,—Thou mayst trust the messenger. He will lead thee in safety to one who waits for thee. Delay not; danger is around thee.
>
> > Thine, Ernest.

Ah, here! so near me! Hope springs anew within my heart. Yes, I will go. Homeless, friendless no more! Happy Zara! joy now awaits thee. Yet stay!—my promise to Bernardo! I cannot leave him thus in danger, and alone. What shall I do? Oh, Ernest, where art thou now?

Ernest [*throwing off disguise, and kneeling before her*]. Here, dearest Zara! here at thy feet, to offer thee a true heart's fond devotion. To thee I owe life, liberty, and happiness. Ah, let me thus repay the debt of gratitude. Thy love shalt be my bright reward; my heart thy refuge from all danger now. Wilt thou not trust me?

Zara. Ernest, thou knowest my heart is thine, and that to thee I trust with joy my life and happiness. No vow stands now between us. I am thine.

Ernest. Then let us hence. All is prepared; thy father shall be saved. This night shall see us on our way to liberty; and in a fairer land we may forget the danger, sorrow, and captivity that have been ours. Come, dearest, let me lead thee.

Zara. I come; and, Ernest, 'mid the joy and bright hopes of the future, let us not forget the sorrow and the sacrifice that hath won for us this happiness; and mayst thou ne'er regret the hour that gave to thee the love of the Moorish maiden, Zara.

CURTAIN

64

THE GREEK SLAVE

CHARACTERS

Constantine *Prince betrothed to Irene*.

Queen Zelneth *His Mother*.

Irene *The Greek Princess*.

Ione *The Greek Slave*.

Helon *A Priest*.

Rienzi *A Traitor*.

SCENE FIRST

[*Apartment in the palace of* Irene. Irene, *reclining upon a divan.*]

Irene. How strange a fate is mine! Young, fair, and highborn, I may not choose on whom I will bestow my love! Betrothed to a prince whom I have never seen; compelled to honor and obey one whom my heart perchance can never love, alas! alas!

And yet, they tell me that Constantine is noble, brave, and good. What more can I desire? Ah, if he do but love me I shall be content [*noise without; she rises*]. Hark! 'tis his messenger approaching with letters from the queen, his mother. I will question this ambassador, and learn yet more of this young prince, my future husband [*seats herself with dignity*].

[*Enter* Rienzi. *Kneels, presenting a letter.*

Rienzi. The queen, my mistress, sends thee greeting, lady, and this scroll. May it please thee, read. I await your pleasure.

Irene [*takes the letter and reads*]. My lord, with a woman's curiosity, I fain would ask thee of thy prince, whose fate the gods have linked with mine. Tell me, is he tender, true, and noble? Answer truly, I do command thee.

Rienzi. Lady, he is tender as a woman, gentle as thy heart could wish, just and brave as a king should ever be. The proudest lady in all Greece were well matched with our noble Constantine.

Irene. And is he fair to look upon? Paint me his likeness, if thou canst.

Rienzi. I can but ill perform that office. Thou must see if thou wouldst rightly know him. The gods have blessed him with a fair and stately form, a noble face, dark locks, and a king-like brow that well befits the crown that rests upon it. This is he, our brave young prince; one to honor, lady; one to trust and—love.

Irene. 'Tis a noble man thou hast painted. One more question and thou mayst retire. Hath he ever spoken of her who is to be his wife? Nay, why do I fear to ask thee? Does he love her?

66

Rienzi. Lady, I beg thee ask me not. Who could fail to love when once he had looked upon thee?

Irene. Thou canst not thus deceive me. Answer truly: What doth he think of this betrothal and approaching marriage?

Rienzi. He hath not seen thee, princess, knows of thee nothing save that thou art beautiful, and one day to become his wife. But he is young, and hath no wish to wed, and even his mother's prayers have failed to win his free consent to this most cherished plan, that by uniting thy fair kingdom unto his, he can gain power over other lands and beautify our own.

Irene. Perchance his heart is given to another. Has no fair Grecian maiden won the love he cannot offer me?

Rienzi. Nay, lady. He loves nought but his mother, his subjects, and his native land. But soon we trust, when thou art by his side, a deeper love will wake within him, and thou wilt be dearer than country, home, or friends.

Irene. 'Tis well; thou mayst retire. I will send answer by thee to thy queen, and seek some gift that may be worthy her acceptance. And now, adieu! [Rienzi *bows and retires.*] He does not love me, then, and I must wed a cold and careless lord. And yet—so tender to all others, he could not be unkind to me alone.

Oh, that I could win his love unknown, and then when truly mine, to cast away the mask, and be myself again. Stay! let me think. Ah, yes; I see a way. Surely the gods have sent the thought! I will disguise me as a slave, and as a gift sent to his mother, I can see and learn to know him well. I will return with the ambassador, Rienzi. I spake to him of a gift. He little thinks in the veiled slave he shall bear away, the princess is concealed. Yes, Constantine, as a nameless girl will Irene win thy heart; and when as a wife she stands beside thee, thou shalt love her for herself alone.

[*Tableau.*

CURTAIN

67

SCENE SECOND

[*A room in the palace of* The Queen. The Queen *alone.*]

Queen. Why comes he not? They told me that our ambassador to the Princess Irene had returned, and bore a gift for me. Would that it were a picture of herself! They say she is wondrous fair; and could my wayward son but gaze upon her, his heart might yet be won. [*Enter* Irene, *disguised as the slave,* Ione.] Ah, a stranger! Who art thou?

[Ione *kneels and presents a letter.*

Queen [*reads the letter*]. Ah, welcome! Thy mistress tells me she hath chosen from among her train the fairest and most faithful of her slaves, as a gift for me. With thanks do I accept thee. Lift thy veil, child, that I may see how our maidens do compare with thee. [Ione *lifts her veil.* The Queen *gazes in surprise at her beauty.*] Thou art too beautiful to be a slave. What is thy name?

Ione. Ione; may it please thee, lady.

Queen. 'Tis a fit name for one so fair; and thy country, maiden?

Ione. With the princess, my kind mistress, have I dwelt for many happy years; and honored by her choice now offer my poor services to thee.

Queen. What canst thou do, Ione? Thou art too fair and delicate to bear the heavy water-urn or gather fruit.

Ione. I can weave garlands, lady; touch the harp, and sing sweet songs; can bear thee wine, and tend thy flowers. I can be true and faithful, and no task will be too hard for thy grateful slave, Ione.

Queen. Thou shalt find a happy home with me, and never grieve for thy kind mistress. And now, listen while I tell thee what thy hardest task shall be. I will confide in thee, Ione, for thou art no common slave, but a true and gentle woman whom I can trust and love. Thou hath heard thy lady is betrothed to my most noble son; and yet, I grieve to say, he loves her not. Nay, in the struggle 'gainst his heart, hath lost all gayety and strength, and even the name Irene will chase

68

the smile away. He loves no other, yet will not offer her his hand when the heart that should go with it feels no love for her who is to be his wife. I honor this most noble feeling; yet could he know the beauty and the worth of thy fair lady, he yet might love. Thou shalt tell him this: all the kind deeds she hath done, the gentle words she hath spoken; all her loveliness and truth thou shalt repeat; sing thou the songs she loved; weave round his cups the flowers she wears; and strive most steadfastly to gain a place within his heart for love and Lady Irene. Canst thou, wilt thou do this, Ione?

Ione. Dear lady, all that my poor skill can do shall yet be tried. I will not rest till he shall love my mistress as she longs to be beloved.

Queen. If thou canst win my son to health and happiness again, thou shalt be forever my most loved, most trusted friend. The gods bless thee, child, and give thy work success! Now rest thee here. I will come ere long to lead thee to the prince.

[*Exit* The Queen.

Ione. All goes well; and what an easy task is mine! To minister to him whom I already love; to sing to him, weave garlands for his brow, and tell him of the thoughts stirring within my heart. Yes, I most truly long to see him whom all love and honor. The gods be with me, and my task will soon be done.

CURTAIN

SCENE THIRD

[*Another room in the palace.* Constantine, *sad and alone.*]

Con. Another day is well-nigh passed, and nearer draws the fate I dread. Why must I give up all the bright dreams of my youth, and wed a woman whom I cannot love?

They tell me she is young and fair, but I seek more than that in her who is to pass her life beside me. Youth and beauty fade, but a noble woman's love can never die. Oh, Irene, if thou couldst know how hard a thing it is to take thee, princess though thou art! [*Enter* Ione.] Ah, lady, thou hast mistaken thy way! Let me lead thee to the queen's apartments.

Ione. Nay, my lord; I have come from her. She bid me say it was her will that I, her slave, should strive with my poor skill to while away the time till she could join thee.

Con. Thou, a slave? By the gods! methought it was some highborn lady,—nay, even the Princess Irene herself, seeking the queen, my mother.

Ione. She was my mistress, and bestowed me as a gift upon the queen. This scroll is from her hand. May it please thee, read it [*kneels and presents letter*].

Con. Rise, fair maiden! I would rather listen to thy voice. May I ask thee to touch yon harp? I am weary, and a gentle strain will sooth my troubled spirit. Stay! let me place it for thee.

[*Prince moves the harp and gazes upon* Ione *as she sings and plays.*

The wild birds sing in the orange groves,
And brightly bloom the flowers;
The fair earth smiles 'neath a summer sky
Through the joyous fleeting hours.
But oh! in the slave girl's lonely heart,
Sad thoughts and memories dwell,

And tears fall fast as she mournfully sings,
Home, dear home, farewell!

Though the chains they bind be all of flowers,
Where no hidden thorn may be,
Still the free heart sighs 'neath its fragrant bonds,
And pines for its liberty.
And sweet, sad thoughts of the joy now gone,
In the slave girl's heart shall dwell,
As she mournfully sings to her sighing harp,
Native land, native land, farewell!

Con. 'Tis a plaintive song. Is it thine own lot thou art mourning? If so, thou art a slave no longer.

Ione. Nay, my lord. It was one my Lady Irene loved, and thus I thought would please thee.

Con. Then never sing it more,—speak not her name! Nay, forgive me if I pain thee. She was thy mistress, and thou didst love her. Was she kind to thee? By what name shall I call thee?

Ione. Ione, your Highness. Ah, yes; she was too kind. She never spake a cruel word, nor chid me for my many faults. Never can I love another as I loved my gentle mistress.

Con. And is she very fair? Has she no pride, no passion or disdain to mar her loveliness? She is a princess; is she a true and tender woman too?

Ione. Though a princess, 'neath her royal robes there beats a warm, true heart, faithful and fond, longing to be beloved and seeking to be worthy such great joy when it shall come. Thou ask'st me of her beauty. Painters place her face among their fairest works, and sculptors carve her form in marble. Yes, she is beautiful; but 'tis not that thou wouldst most care for. Couldst thou only know her!— pardon, but I think thou couldst not bear so cold a heart within thy breast as now.

Con. Ah, do not cease! say on! There is that in the music of thy voice that soothes and comforts me. Come, sit beside me, fair Ione, and I will tell thee why I do not love thy princess.

71

Ione. You do forget, my lord, I am a slave; I will kneel here.

[*Prince reclines upon a couch.* Ione *kneels beside him.*

Con. Listen! From a boy I have been alone; no loving sister had I, no gentle friend,—only cold councillors or humble slaves. My mother was a queen, and 'mid the cares of State, tho' fondly loving me, her only son, could find no time to win me from my lonely life.

Thus, tho' dwelling 'neath a palace roof with every wish supplied, I longed most fondly for a friend. And now, ere long, a crown will rest upon my head, a nation bend before me as their king. And now more earnestly than ever do I seek one who can share with me the joys and cares of my high lot,—a woman true and noble, to bless me with her love.

Ione. And could not the Princess Irene be to thee all thou hast dreamed?

Con. I fear I cannot love her. They told me she was beautiful and highborn; and when I sought to learn yet more, 'twas but to find she was a cold, proud woman, fit to be a queen, but not a loving wife. Thus I learned to dread the hour when I must wed. Yet 'tis my mother's will; my country's welfare calls for the sacrifice, and I must yield myself.

Ione. They who told thee she was proud and cold do all speak falsely. Proud she is to those who bow before her but to gain some honor for themselves, and cold to such as love her for her royalty alone. But if a fond and faithful heart, and a soul that finds its happiness in noble deeds can make a queen, Irene is worthy of the crown she will wear. And now, if it please thee, I will seek the garden; for thy mother bid me gather flowers for the feast. Adieu, my lord! [*She bows, her veil falls*; Constantine *hands it to her.*] Nay, kings should not bend to serve a slave, my lord.

Con. I do forget myself most strangely. There, take thy veil, and leave me [*turns aside*]. Nay, forgive me if I seem unkind, but I cannot treat thee as a slave. Come, I will go with thee to the garden; thou art too fair to wander unprotected and alone. Come, Ione [*leads her out*].

CURTAIN

72

SCENE FOURTH

[*The gardens of the palace.* Ione *weaving a garland.*]

Ione. The rose is Love's own flower, and I will place it in the wreath I weave for thee, O Constantine! Would I could bring it to thy heart as easily! And yet, methinks, if all goes on as now, the slave Ione will ere long win a prince's love. He smiles when I approach, and sighs when I would leave him; listens to my songs, and saves the withered flowers I gave him days ago. How gentle and how kind! Ah, noble Constantine, thou little thinkest the slave thou art smiling on is the "proud, cold" Princess Irene, who will one day show thee what a fond, true wife she will be to thee [*sings*].

[*Enter* Helon; *kneels to* Ione.

Ione. Helon, my father's friend! thou here! Ah, hush! Betray me not! I am no princess now. Rise, I do beseech thee! Kneel not to me.

Helon. Dear lady, why this secrecy? What dost thou here, disguised, in the palace where thou art soon to reign a queen?

Ione. Hark! is all still? Yes; none are nigh! Speak low. I'll tell thee all. Thou knowest the young prince loves me not,—nay, do not sigh; I mean the princess, not the slave Ione, as I now call myself. Well, I learned this, and vowed to win the heart he could not give; and so in this slave's dress I journeyed hither with Rienzi, the ambassador, as a gift unto the queen.

Thus, as a poor and nameless slave, I seek to win the noble Constantine to life and love. Dost understand my plot, and wilt thou aid me, Father Helon?

Helon. 'Tis a strange thought! None but a woman would have planned it. Yes, my child, I will aid thee, and thou yet shall gain the happiness thy true heart well deserves. We will talk of this yet more anon. I came hither to see the prince. They told me he was pale and ill, in sorrow for his hated lot. Say, is this so?

Ione. Ah, yes, most true; and I am cause of all this sorrow. Father, tell me, cannot I by some great deed give back his health, and never

73

have the grief of knowing that he suffered because I was his bride? How can I avert this fate? I will do all, bear all, if he may be saved.

Helon. Grieve not, my child; he will live, and learn to love thee fondly. The cares of a kingdom are too much for one so young; but he would have happiness throughout his native land, and toiling for the good of others he hath hidden his sorrow in his own heart, and pined for tenderness and love. Thou hast asked if thou couldst save him. There is one hope, if thou canst find a brave friend that fears no danger when a good work leads him on. Listen, my daughter! In a deep and lonely glen, far beyond the palace gates, there grows an herb whose magic power 'tis said brings new life and strength to those who wreathe it round their head in slumber. Yet none dare seek the spot, for spirits are said to haunt the glen, and not a slave in all the palace but grows pale at mention of the place. I am old and feeble, or I had been there long ere this. And now, my child, who canst thou send?

Ione. I will send one who fears not spirit or demon; one who will gladly risk e'en life itself for the brave young prince.

Helon. Blessed be the hand that gathers, thrice blessed be he who dares the dangers of the way. Bring hither him thou speakest of. I would see him.

Ione. She stands before thee. Nay, start not, Father. *I* will seek the dreaded glen and gather there the magic flowers that may bring health to Constantine and happiness to me. I will away; bless, and let me go.

Helon. Thou, a woman delicate and fair! Nay, nay, it must not be, my child! Better he should die than thou shouldst come to harm. I cannot let thee go.

Ione. Thou canst not keep me now. Thou hast forgot I am a slave, and none may guess beneath this veil a princess is concealed. I will take my water-urn, and with the other slaves pass to the spring beyond the city gates; then glide unseen into the haunted glen. Now, tell me how looks the herb, that I may know it.

Helon. 'Tis a small, green plant that blossoms only by the broad, dark stream, dashing among the rocks that fill the glen. But let me once again implore thee not to go. Ah, fatal hour when first I told thee! 'Tis sending thee to thy death! Stay, stay, my child, or let me go with thee.

Ione. It cannot be; do thou remain, and if I come not back ere set of sun, do thou come forth to seek me. Tell Constantine I loved him, and so farewell. I return successful, or I return no more.

[Ione *rushes out.*

Helon. Thou brave and noble one to dare so much for one who loves thee not! I'll go and pray the gods to watch above thee, and bring thee safely back.

[*Exit* Helon.

CURTAIN

SCENE FIFTH

[*A terrace beside the palace. Enter* Constantine.]

Con. Why comes she not? I watched her slender form when with the other slaves she went forth to the fountain yonder. I knew her by the rosy veil and snow-white arm that bore the water-urn. The morning sun shone brightly on the golden hair, and seemed more beautiful for resting there; and now 'tis nearly set, and yet she comes not. Why should I grieve because my mother's slave forgets me? Shame on thee, Constantine! How weak and childish have I grown! This fever gives no rest when Ione is not here to sing sweet songs, and cheer the weary hours. Ah, she comes! [*Enter* Ione *with basket of flowers.*] Where hast thou been, Ione? The long day passed so slowly, and I missed thee sadly from my side. But thou art pale; thy locks are damp! What has chanced to thee? Speak, I beseech thee!

Ione. 'Tis nothing; calm thyself, my lord. I am well, and bring thee from the haunted glen the magic flowers whose power I trust will win thee health and happiness. May it please thee to accept them [*kneels, and gives the flowers*].

Con. Thou, thou, Ione? Hast thou been to that fearful spot, where mortal foot hath feared to tread? The gods be blessed, thou art safe again! How can I thank thee? Ah, why didst thou risk so much for my poor life? It were not worth the saving if thine were lost.

Ione. My lord, a loving nation looks to thee for safety and protection. I am but a feeble woman, and none would grieve if I were gone; none weep for the friendless slave, Ione.

Con. Oh, say not thus! Tears would be shed for thee, and one heart would grieve for her who risked so much for him. Speak not of death or separation, for I cannot let thee go.

Ione. I will not leave thee yet, till I have won thy lost health back. The old priest, Helon, bid me seek the herbs, and bind them in a garland for thy brow. If thou wilt place it there, and rest awhile, I am repaid.

Con. If thy hand gave it, were it deadly poison I would place it there.

76

Now sing, Ione; thy low sweet voice will bring me pleasant dreams, and the healing sleep will be the deeper with thy music sounding in mine ears.

[*The prince reclines upon the terrace.* Ione *weaves a garland and sings.*

Flowers, sweet flowers, I charge thee well,
O'er the brow where ye bloom cast a healing spell;
From the shadowy glen where spirits dwell,
I have borne thee here, thy power to tell.
 Flowers, pale flowers, o'er the brow where ye lie,
Cast thy sweetest breath ere ye fade and die.

[Ione *places the garland on the head of the prince, who falls asleep. She sits beside him softly singing.*

CURTAIN

SCENE SIXTH

[The Queen's *apartment*. The Queen *alone*.]

Queen. 'Tis strange what power this slave hath gained o'er Constantine. She hath won him back to health again, and never have I seen so gay a smile upon his lips as when she stood beside him in the moonlight singing to her harp. And yet, tho' well and strong again, he takes no interest in his native land. He comes no more to council hall or feast, but wanders 'mong his flowers with Ione. How can I rouse him to the danger that is near! The Turkish sultan and his troops are on their way to conquer Greece, and he, my Constantine, who should be arming for the fight, sits weaving garlands with the lovely slave girl! Ah, a thought hath seized me! Why cannot she who hath such power o'er him rouse up with noble words the brave heart slumbering in his breast? I hear her light step in the hall. Ione, Ione,—come hither! I would speak with thee.

[*Enter* Ione.

Ione. Your pleasure, dearest lady.

Queen. Ione, thou knowest how I love thee for the brave deeds thou hast done. Thou hast given health unto my son, hath won him back to happiness. Thou hast conquered his aversion to the princess, and he will gladly wed her when the hour shall come. Is it not so?

Ione. Dear lady, that I cannot tell thee. He never breathes her name, and if I speak of her as thou hast bid me, he but sighs, and grows more sad; and yet I trust, nay, I well know that when he sees her he will gladly give his hand to one who loves him as the princess will. Then do not grieve, but tell thy slave how she may serve thee.

Queen. Oh, Ione, if thou couldst wake him from the quiet dream that seems to lie upon his heart. His country is in danger, and he should be here to counsel and command. Go, tell him this in thine own gentle words; rouse him to his duty, and thou shalt see how brave a heart is there. Thou hast a wondrous power to sadden or to cheer. Oh, use it well, and win me back my noble Constantine! Canst thou do this, Ione?

Ione. I will; and strive most earnestly to do thy bidding. But of what danger didst thou speak? No harm to him, I trust?

Queen. The Turkish troops are now on their way to carry woe and desolation into Greece, and he, the prince, hath taken no part in the councils. His nobles mourn at his strange indifference, and yet he heeds them not.

I know not why, but some new happiness hath come to him, and all else is forgot. But time is passing. I will leave thee to thy work, and if thou art successful, thou wilt have won a queen's most fervent gratitude. Adieu, my child!

[*Exit* The Queen.

Ione. Yes, Constantine, thy brave heart shall awake; and when thy country is once safe again, I'll come to claim the love that now I feel is mine.

[*Exit* Ione.

CURTAIN

SCENE SEVENTH

[*Apartment in the palace. Enter* Ione *with sword and banner.*]

Ione. Now may the gods bless and watch above thee, Constantine; give strength to thine arm, courage to thy heart, and victory to the cause for which thou wilt venture all. Ah, could I but go with thee, thy shield would then be useless, for with mine own breast would I shelter thee, and welcome there the arrows meant for thee.

He comes; now let me rouse him from this dream, and try my power o'er his heart.

[*Enter* Constantine.

Con. What high thoughts stirring in thy heart hath brought the clear light to thine eye, Ione, the bright glow to thy cheek? What mean these arms? Wouldst thou go forth to meet the Turks? Thy beauty would subdue them sooner than the sword thou art gazing on so earnestly.

Ione. Thou hast bade me speak, my lord, and I obey; but pardon thy slave if in her wish to serve she seem too bold. Thy mother and thy subjects wonder at thy seeming indifference when enemies are nigh. Thine army waits for thee to lead them forth; thy councillors sit silent, for their prince is gone. While grief and terror reign around, he is wandering 'mong his flowers, or listening to the music of his harp. Ah, why is this? What hath befallen thee? Thou art no longer pale and feeble, yet there seems a spell set on thee. Ah, cast it off, and show them that thou hast no fear.

Con. I am no coward, Ione; but there is a spell upon me. 'Tis a holy one, and the chain that holds me here I cannot break,—for it is *love*. I have lost the joy I once took in my subjects and my native land, and am content to sit beside thee, and listen to the music of thy voice.

Ione. Then let that voice arouse thee. Oh, fling away the chain that keeps thee from thy duty, and be again the noble prince who thought but of his people. Oh, let me plead for those who sorrow for thy care, and here let me implore thee to awaken from thy dream and be thyself again [*she kneels*].

Con. Oh, not to me! Rise, I beseech thee, rise! Thou hast led me to my duty; I will obey thee.

Ione. I would have thee gird on thy sword, and with shield upon thine arm, and banner in thy hand, go forth and conquer like a king. Show those who doubt thee that their fears are false,—that thou art worthy of their love. Lead forth thy troops, and save thy country from the woe that now draws nigh. Victory surely will be theirs when thou shalt lead them on.

Con. Give me my sword, unfurl my banner, and say farewell. I will return victorious, or no more. Thy voice hath roused me from my idle but most lovely dream, and thy brave words shall cheer me on till I have won the honor of my people back. Pity and forgive my fault; and ah, remember in thy prayers one who so passionately loves thee. Farewell! farewell!

[*Kisses her robe and rushes out.* Ione *sinks down.*

CURTAIN

SCENE EIGHTH

[*On the battlements.* Ione, *watching the battle.*]

Ione. The battle rages fiercely at the city gates, and the messengers are fearful of defeat. I cannot rest while Constantine is in such peril. Let me watch here and pray for him. Ah, I can see his white plume waving in the thickest of the fight, where the blows fall heaviest and the danger is most great. The gods guard him in this fearful hour! See how small the brave band grows; they falter and retreat. One blow now bravely struck may turn the tide of battle. It shall be done! I will arm the slaves now in the palace, and lead them on to victory or death. We may win—and if *not*, I shall die in saving thee, Constantine!

[Ione *rushes out.*

CURTAIN

SCENE NINTH

[*The castle terrace. Enter* Constantine.]

Con. The victory is ours, and Greece again is free, thanks to the gods, and to the brave unknown who led on my slaves, and saved us when all hope seemed gone. Who could have been the fearless stranger? Like an avenging spirit came the mysterious leader, carrying terror and destruction to the Turkish ranks. My brave troops rallied and we won the day. Yet when I sought him, he was gone, and none could tell me where. He hath won my deepest gratitude, and the honor of all Greece for this brave deed.

But where is Ione? Why comes she not to bid me welcome home? Ah, could she know that thoughts of her gave courage to my heart, and strength to my weak arm, and led me on that I might be more worthy her! Ah, yonder comes the stranger; he may not think to see me here. I will step aside.

[Constantine *retires. Enter* Ione *in armor, bearing sword.*

Ione. The gods be thanked! the brave young prince hath conquered. From the flying Turk I won his banner back, and now my task is done. I must fling by this strange disguise and be myself again. I must bind up my wound and seek to rest, for I am faint and weary. Ah, what means this sudden dimness of mine eyes, this faintness—can it be death? 'T is welcome,—Constantine, it is for thee!

[Ione *faints*; Constantine *rushes in.*

Con. Ione, Ione, look up and listen to the blessings of my grateful heart for all thou hast dared and done for me. So pale, so still! Ah, must she die now I have learned to love so fervently and well? Ione, awake!

[Ione *rouses.*

Ione. Pardon this weakness; I will retire, my lord.

Con. Ah, do not leave me till I have poured out my gratitude. My country owes its liberty to thee: then let me here before thee offer up my country's thanks, and tell thee what my heart hath striven to hide. Dear Ione, listen, I do beseech thee! [*Kneels.*]

Ione. My lord, remember Lady Irene.

Con. [*starting up*]. Why comes she thus between my happiness and me? Why did she send thee hither? Thou hast made the chain that binds her to me heavier to be borne; the sorrow of my heart more bitter still. Nay, do not weep. I will be calm. Thou art pale and faint, Ione,—lean thus on me.

Ione. Nay, leave me; I cannot listen to thee. Go, I pray thee, go!

Con. Not till thou hast pardoned me. I have made thee weep, and every tear that falls reproaches me for my rash words. Forget them, and forgive me.

Ione. Ask not forgiveness of thy slave, my lord. 'Tis I who have offended. And think not thus of Lady Irene, who in her distant home hath cherished tender thoughts of one whom all so honored. Think of her grief when she shall find thee cold and careless, and shall learn that he who should most love and cherish, deems her but a burden, and hates the wife whom he hath vowed to wed. Ah, think of this, and smile no more upon the slave who may not listen to her lord.

Con. Thou art right, Ione. I will obey thee, and seek to hide my sorrow within my lonely breast. Teach me to love thy mistress as I ought, and I will sacrifice each selfish wish, and be more worthy thy forgiveness, and a little place within thy heart. Trust me, I will speak no more of my unhappy love, and will seek thee only when thine own voice bids me come.

The sunlight of thy presence is my truest joy, and banishment from thee the punishment my wilful heart deserves. Rest here, Ione, and weep for me no more. I am happy if thou wilt but smile again. Farewell, and may the gods forever bless thee! [*Kisses her robe, and rushes out.*]

CURTAIN

84

SCENE TENTH

[*A gallery in the palace. Enter* Ione *with flowers.*]

Ione. How desolate and dreary all hath grown! The garden once so bright hath lost its beauty now, for Constantine no longer walks beside me. The palace rooms seem sad and lonely, for his voice no longer echoes there, and the music of his harp is never heard. His pale face haunts me through all my waking hours, and his mournful eyes look on me in my dreams. But soon his sorrow all shall cease, for nearer draws the day when Princess Irene comes to claim the heart so hardly won, and will by constancy and love so faithfully reward. Hark! I hear a step. It is Rienzi. How shall I escape,—my veil is in the garden! He knows me and will discover all. Stay! this curtain shall conceal me [*hides within the drapery*].

[*Enter* Rienzi *stealthily.*

Rienzi. How! not here? I told the messenger to meet me in the gallery that leads from the garden. Curses on him! he hath delayed, and were I discovered in this part of the palace, all might be betrayed. I'll wait, and if he comes not, I'll bear the message to the friends myself, and tell the bold conspirators we meet to-night near the haunted glen, to lay yet farther plans. We must rid the kingdom of the prince, who will be made ere long our king, for his bridal with the Princess Irene draws more near. But ere the royal crown shall rest upon his brow, that head shall be laid low. The queen will soon follow her young son, and then we'll seize the kingdom and rule it as we will. Hark! methought I heard a sound. I may be watched. I'll stay no longer, but seek the place myself [*steals out and disappears in the garden*].

[Ione *comes from her hiding-place.*

Ione. Surely the gods have sent me to watch above thee, Constantine, and save thee from the danger that surrounds thee. I will haste to tell him all I have discovered. Yet, no! Rienzi may escape, and I can charge none other with the crime. They meet near the haunted glen, and not a slave would follow even his brave prince to that dark spot. How can I aid him to discover those who seek to do him harm? Stay! I will go alone. Once have I dared the dangers of the way to save thy life, Constantine; again I'll tread the fearful path, and watch the traitors at their evil work. It shall be done! I will dare all, and fail not, falter not, till thou who art dearer to me than life itself art safe again.

[*Exit.*

CURTAIN

SCENE ELEVENTH

[*A wood near the haunted glen.* Ione *shrouded in white glides in and conceals herself among the trees. Enter* Rienzi.]

Rienzi [*looking fearfully about*]. 'Tis a wild and lonely spot, and 'tis said strange spirits have been seen to wander here. Why come they not? 'Tis past the hour, and I who stand undaunted when the fiercest battle rages round me, now tremble with strange fear in this dim spot. Shame on thee, Rienzi, there is nought to fear [*opens a scroll and reads*]. Here are their names, all pledged to see the deed accomplished. 'Tis a goodly list and Constantine must fall when foes like these are round him. [Ione *appears within the glen.*

Ha! methought I heard a sound! Nay, 'twas my foolish fancy. Spirits, I defy thee!

Ione. Beware! Beware!

Rienzi. Ye gods, what's that? It was a voice. [*Rushes wildly towards the glen, sees* Ione, *drops scroll and dagger.*] 'Tis a spirit! The gods preserve me, I will not stay! [*Exit in terror.*]

[*Enter* Ione.

Ione. Saved! saved! Here are the traitors' names, and here Rienzi's dagger to prove my story true. Now hence with all my speed, no time is to be lost! These to thee, Constantine, and joy unfailing to my own fond heart.

[*Exit* Ione.]

CURTAIN

SCENE TWELFTH

[*Apartment in the palace. Enter* Constantine.]

Con. This little garland of pale, withered flowers is all now left me of Ione, faded like my own bright hopes, broken like my own sad heart. Yet still I cherish it, for her dear hand wove the wreath, and her soft eyes smiled above the flowers as she twined them for my brow. Those happy days are passed; she comes no more, but leaves me sorrowing and alone. And yet 'tis better so. The princess comes to claim my hand, and then 'twill be a sin to watch Ione, to follow her unseen, and listen to her voice when least she thinks me near. The gods give me strength to bear my trial worthily, and suffer silently the greatest sorrow life can give,—that of losing her [*leans sadly upon the harp*].

[*Enter* Ione.

Ione. My lord—He does not hear me, how bitter and how deep must be his grief, when the voice that most he loves falls thus unheeded on his ear. My lord—

Con. [*starting*]. And thou art really here? Ah, Ione, I have longed for thee most earnestly. Ah, forgive me! In my joy I have disobeyed, and told the happiness thy presence brings. What wouldst thou with me?

Ione. My lord, I have strange tidings for thine ear.

Con. Oh, tell me not the Princess Irene hath arrived!

Ione. Nay, 'tis not that. I have learned the secret of a fearful plot against thy life. Rienzi, and a band of other traitors, seek to win thy throne and take the life of their kind prince.

Con. It cannot be, Ione! They could not raise their hands 'gainst one who hath striven for their good. They cannot wish the life I would so gladly have lain down to save them. Who told thee this, Ione? I cannot—no, I will not think they could prove so ungrateful unto their prince.

Ione. I cannot doubt the truth of this, my lord, for one whose word I trust learned it, and followed to the haunted glen, there saw Rienzi, whose guilty conscience drove him from the place, leaving behind this scroll whereon are all the traitors' names. And this dagger,—'tis his own, as thou mayst see [*shows dagger and scroll*].

Con. I can no longer doubt; but I had rather have felt the dagger in my heart than such a wound as this. The names are few; I fear them not, and will ere long show them a king may pardon all save treachery like this. But tell the name of thy brave friend who hath discovered this deep treason, and let me offer some reward to one who hath watched above me with such faithful care.

Ione. Nay, my lord, no gift, no thanks are needed. 'Tis a true and loving subject, who is well rewarded if his king be safe.

Con. Thou canst not thus deceive me. It was thine own true heart that dared so much to save my life. Oh, Ione, why wilt thou make me love thee more by deeds like these,—why make the sorrow heavier to bear, the parting sadder still?

Ione. Thou dost forget, my lord, I have but done my duty. May it please thee, listen to a message I bear thee from the queen.

Con. Say on. I will gladly listen to thy voice while yet I may.

Ione. She bid me tell thee that to-morrow, ere the sun shall set, the Princess Irene will be here. [Constantine *starts and turns aside*.] Forgive me that I pain thee, but I must obey. Yet, farther: thy bride hath sent her statue as a gift to thee, and thou wilt find it in the queen's pavilion. She bid me say she prayed thee to go look upon it, and remember there thy solemn vow.

Con. Oh, Ione, could she send none but thee to tell me this? To hear it from thy lips but makes the tidings heavier to bear. Canst thou bid me go, and vow to love one whom I have learned to hate? Canst thou bid me leave thee for a fate like this?

Ione. My lord, thou art soon to be a king; then for thy country's sake, remember thy hand is plighted to the princess, and let no kindly thoughts of a humble slave keep thy heart from its solemn duty.

Con. I am no king,—'tis I who am the slave, and thou, Ione, are more to me than country, home, or friends. Nay, do not turn away,—think only of the love I bear thee, and listen to my prayer.

89

Ione. I must not listen. Hast thou so soon forgot the vow thou made that no word of love should pass thy lips? Remember, 'tis a slave who stands before thee.

Con. Once more thou shalt listen to me, Ione, and then I will be still forever. Thou shalt be my judge, thy lips *shall* speak my fate. I cannot love the princess. Wouldst thou bid me vow to cherish her while my heart is wholly thine? Wouldst thou ask me to pass through life beside her with a false vow on my lips, and, with words of love I do not feel, conceal from her the grief of my divided heart? Must I give up all the bright dreams of a happier lot, and feel that life is but a bitter struggle, a ceaseless longing but for thee? Rather bid me to forget the princess and bind with Love's sweet chains the slave unto my side,—my bride forever.

Ione. The *slave* Ione can never be thy bride, and thou art bound by solemn vows to wed the Princess Irene. My duty and thine honor are more precious than a poor slave's love. Banish all thoughts of her, and prove thyself a faithful lord unto the wife who comes now trustingly to thee. Ask thine own heart if life could be a bitter pilgrimage, when a sacrifice like this had been so nobly made. A tender wife beside thee, a mother's blessing on thy head,—oh, were not this a happier fate than to enjoy a short, bright dream of love, but to awake and find thy heart's peace gone, thy happiness forever fled; to see the eyes that once looked reverently upon thee now turned aside, and lips that spoke but tender words now whisper scornfully of broken vows thou wert not brave enough to keep. Forgive me, but I cannot see the prince so false to his own noble heart. Cast off this spell; forget me, and Irene shall win thee back to happiness.

Con. Never! All her loveliness can never banish the pure, undying love I bear to thee. Oh, Ione, canst thou doubt its truth, when I obey thee now and prove how great thy power o'er my heart hath grown? Oh, let the sacrifice win from *thee* one gentle thought, one kind remembrance of him whose life thou hast made so beautiful for a short hour. And in my loneliness, sweet memories of thee shall cheer and gladden, and I will bear all for thy dear sake. And now farewell. Forgive if I have grieved thee, and at parting grant me one token to the silent love that henceforth must lie unseen within my heart. Farewell, Ione! [*He kisses her.*]

Ione [*falling at his feet*]. Ah, forgive me,—here let me seek thy pardon for the grief I have brought thee. May all the happiness that earth can bring be ever thine. But, if all others should forsake thee, in thine hour of sorrow remember there is one true heart that cannot change. Oh, may the gods bless thee! 'Tis my last wish, last prayer [*weeps*]. Farewell!

Con. Stay! I would claim from thee one little word which hath the power to brighten e'en my sorrow. I have never asked thee, for I thought my heart had read it in thine eyes that looked so kindly on me; in the lips that spoke such gentle words of hope. But ah! tell me now at parting dost thou *love* me, dear Ione?

Ione. I do, most fondly, truly love thee.

Con. Ione, thy voice hath been a holy spell to win me to my duty. Thy love shall keep me pure and faithful, till we meet above. Farewell!

Ione. Farewell!—and oh, remember how I have loved thee; and may the memory of all I have borne for thee win thy pardon for any wrong I may have done thee. The princess will repay the grief the slave hath caused thy noble heart. Remember Ione, and be true.

[*Exit.*

Con. Gone, gone, now lost to me forever! Remember thee! Ah, how can I ever banish thy dear image from this heart that now hath grown so desolate? I will be true. None shall ever know how hard a struggle hath been mine, that I might still be worthy thee. Yes, Irene, I will strive to love thee, and may the gods give me strength; but Ione, Ione, how can I give thee up! [*Picks up a flower* Ione *has dropped, and puts it in his bosom and goes sadly out.*]

CURTAIN

SCENE THIRTEENTH

[The Queen's *pavilion. A dark curtain hangs before an alcove. Enter* Constantine.]

Con. The hour hath come when I shall gaze upon the form of her who hath cast so dark a shadow o'er my life. Beautiful and young, and blessed with all that makes her worthy to be loved, and yet I fear I have not taught my wilful heart the tenderness I ought.

I fear to draw aside the veil that hides her from me, for I cannot banish the sweet image that forever floats before mine eyes. Ione's soft gaze is on me, and the lips are whispering, "I love thee!" But I have promised to be true,—no thoughts of her must lead me now astray. My fate is here [*approaches the curtain*]. Let me gaze upon it, and think gently of the wife so soon to be mine own. Why do I fear? Courage, my heart! [*He draws aside the curtain, and* Ione, *veiled, appears as a statue upon its pedestal.*] Another veil to raise! How hard the simple deed hath grown. One last sweet thought of thee, Ione, and then I will no longer falter. [*He turns away and bows his head.*]

Ione. Constantine! [*He starts, and gazes in wonder as the statue, casting aside the veil, comes down and kneels.*] Here at thy feet kneels thy hated bride,—the "proud, cold princess," asking thee to pardon all the sorrow she hath given thee. Ah, smile upon me, and forget Ione, who as a slave hath won thy love, but as the princess will repay it,—forgive, and love me still!

Con. Thou, thou Irene,—she whom I so feared to look upon? Ah, no!—thou art Ione, the gentle slave. Say am I dreaming? Why art thou here to make another parting the harder to be borne? Fling by thy crown and be Ione again.

Irene [*rising*]. Listen, Constantine, and I will tell thee all. I am Irene. In my distant home I learned thou didst not love me, and I vowed to win thy heart before I claimed it. Thus, unknown, the proud princess served thee as a slave, and learned to love thee with a woman's fondest faith. I watched above thee that no harm should fall; I cheered and gladdened life for thee, and won the heart I longed for. I knew the sorrow thou wouldst feel, but tried thy faith by asking thee to sacrifice thy love and keep thine honor stainless. Here let me offer up a woman's fondest trust and most undying love. Wilt thou believe, and pardon mine offence? [*Kneels again before him.*]

Con. Not at my feet, Irene!—'tis I who should bend low before thee, asking thy forgiveness. For all thou hast dared for me; for every fearless deed; for every loving thought, all I can lay before thee is a fond and faithful heart, whose reverence and love can never die, but through the pilgrimage of life shall be as true and tender as when I gave it to the slave Ione [*embraces* Irene].

[*Tableau.*

CURTAIN

ION

NOTE TO ION

This play was found too uninteresting for presentation, and was left unfinished, but is here given as a specimen of what the young authors considered *very fine* writing.

The drama was, of course, to end well. Cleon, being free, at once assembles a noble army, returns to conquer Mohammed and release Ion, who weds the lovely Zuleika, becomes king, and "lives happily forever after."

CHARACTERS

Mohammed *The Turk.*

Cleon *Prince of Greece.*

Ion *Son of Cleon.*

Adrastus *A Priest.*

Hafiz *Turkish Envoy.*

Hassan *A Slave.*

Murad *A Slave.*

Abdallah *A Slave.*

Iantha *Wife of Cleon.*

Zuleika *Daughter of Mohammed.*

Medon *A Slave.*

Selim *A Slave.*

SCENE FIRST

[*Room in the palace of* Cleon. Iantha *and* Adrastus.]

Iantha. How wearily the days wear on, and the heavy hours so fraught with doubt press like death upon my aching heart. To the young, the fair, the happy, life is a blissful dream, filled with bright joys; for hope like a star beams on their pathway. But to the grief-worn heart, worn with weary watching, vexed with sad cares, whose hours are filled with fear, and ever thronging sorrows, whose star burns with a dim uncertain light,—oh, weary, weary is the pilgrimage; joyless the present, dark the future; and the sooner all is o'er, the better.

Adrastus. Daughter, thou hast forgot. The radiant star may pale and fade, but He who giveth it its light still liveth. Turn unto Him thy worn and bleeding heart, and comfortless thou shalt not be.

Iantha. Father, I cannot. When I would pray for resignation, words fail me, and my soul is filled with murmuring, while round me throng visions of battle-fields and death. Ever comes before me the form of Cleon,—no longer bright and beautiful as when, burning with hope and confidence in his high calling, he went forth to conquer or to die; but fallen, bleeding, perhaps dead, or a captive in the dungeon of the pagan, doomed to waste in hopeless misery the long years of his manhood. And my boy,—what will be his fate? Father, can I think on this and pray?

Adrastus. 'Tis hard, Iantha; but to His aid alone canst thou look up to save thy husband from the horrors of a bloody war. Call on Him, and He, the merciful, will in thy great need be near thee.

[*Enter* Medon.

Medon. A stranger craveth audience.

Iantha [*rushing forward*]. A stranger! Cometh he from my lord?

Medon. I know not, lady; but as a messenger is he clad, and with great haste demandeth speech of thee, saying he bore tidings of great import.

Iantha. Admit him instantly. [*Exit* Medon.] Father, do thou follow, and speed him hither.

Adrastus. I hasten to obey thee. Bear a brave heart, my daughter. I feel that hope is near.

[*Exit* Adrastus.

Iantha [*joyfully*]. Hope,—thrice blessed word!—wilt thou indeed visit this doubting heart once more, and sweeten the cup thou hast so long forsaken? [*Enter* Hafiz.] Welcome! comest thou from my lord? Thy tidings speedily!

Hafiz. To the wife of Cleon, late commander of the rebel Greeks, am I sent to bear tidings of their defeat by Mohammed, now master of all Greece.

Adrastus. And my lord,—the noble Cleon?

Hafiz. Betrayed, defeated, and now lying under sentence of immediate death in the dungeon of the Sultan.

Iantha. Lost! lost! lost! [*Falls fainting on a couch.*]

[*Enter* Adrastus.

Adrastus. Daughter, look up!—there is yet hope. There is no time for rest. Up! rouse thy brave, till now, unconquered heart and cast off this spell. And thou, slave, hence,—away!

[*Exit* Hafiz.

Iantha [*rousing*]. Defeated, imprisoned, condemned,—words unto one heart fraught with such dire despair. Tell me, Father, oh, tell me truly, do I dream?

[*Enter* Ion, *who stands listening.*

Adrastus. 'Tis no dream. The rough soldier did but tell thee in rude speech, what I was hastening in more guarded words to bear thee. 'Tis true; thy lord is in Mohammed's power, a victim to the perfidy of pagans, and doomed unto a speedy death. Nay, Iantha, shrink not, but as a soldier's wife, glory in the death of thy brave knight, dying for his country; and in his martyrdom take to thy soul sweet comfort.

Iantha. Comfort! Oh, man, thou little knowest woman's heart! What to her is glory, when him she loveth is torn from her forever? What to the orphan is the crown of martyrdom, the hero's fame, the praise of nations, the homage of the great? Will they give back the noble dead, heal the broken heart, tear bitter memories from the wounded soul to whom earth is desolate? Nay, Father, nay. Oh, Cleon, would I could die with thee!

Adrastus. This mighty sorrow o'erpowers her reason and will destroy all hope. Iantha, daughter, rouse thyself; let the love thou dost bear thy lord now aid in his deliverance. From the wealth of thy heart's true affection, devise thou some way to save him.

Iantha. Aid me, Father; I have no power of thought. I will trust all to *thee.*

[Ion *approaches.*

Adrastus. I know not what to counsel thee; my life hath ill fitted me to deal with soldiers and with kings. But if some messenger—

Iantha. Nay, it will not serve. None will dare brave the anger of the pagan, and death were the doom of such as approach him other than as a slave. And yet,—perchance he might relent. Oh, were there some true heart, fearless and loving, to aid me now in mine hour of distress! Where can I look for help?

Ion [*coming forward*]. Here, Mother,—*I* will seek the camp of Mohammed.

Iantha. Thou!—my Ion, my only one. No, no; it may not be,—thy tender youth, thy gentle, untried spirit. 'Tis madness e'en to think on!

Ion. Mother, am I not a soldier's son, cradled 'mid warriors? Runs not the blood of heroes in these veins? Are not my father's deeds, his bright, untarnished name, my proud inheritance? What though this tender form is yet untried; what though these arms have never borne the knightly armor? No victor's laurels rest on this youthful brow, and I bear no honored name among the great and glorious of our land; yet, Mother, have I not a father, for whose dear sake I may yet purchase that knighthood for which this young heart glows? Am I not the son of Cleon?

Adrastus. Verily doth a spirit move the boy. Look on him now,

Iantha, and let no weak, unworthy doubt of thine curb the proud spirit that proves him worthy of his sire.

Iantha. My son, my fair, young Ion, thou art all now left my widowed heart. How can I bid thee go! The barbarous pagan will doom thee to a cruel death. How canst thou, an unknown youth, move the fierce heart that hath slain thy sire?

Ion. Fear not, Mother; he who calls me to this glorious mission will protect me. Shall I stand weeping while my father still breathes the air of pagan dungeons; while the base fetters of the infidel rest on his limbs, and his brave followers lie unavenged in their cold, bloody graves; while my country's banner, torn, dishonored, is trampled in the dust,—and he the proud, the brave, till now unconquered defender of that country's honor, lies doomed to an ignominious death? Oh, Mother, bid me go!

Adrastus. Iantha, speak to the boy! Let him not say his *mother* taught him fear.

Iantha. My Ion, go,—strong in thine innocence and faith, go forth upon thy holy mission; and surely He who looketh ever with a loving face on those who put their trust in Him, will in His mercy guard and guide thee [*girds on his sword*]. Farewell! Go,—with thy mother's blessing on thee!

Ion. Now is my heart filled all anew with hope and courage, and I go forth trustingly. Father, thy blessing [*kneels before* Adrastus].

Adrastus. Go, thou self-anointed victim on the altar of thy love. Bless thy pure, faithful heart!

Ion [*rising*]. Farewell! Embrace me, Mother.

Iantha [*pressing* Ion *to her breast*]. Farewell, my Ion. And if the great Father wills it that I look not again on thee in life, into His care do I commit thee. Farewell!

Ion. Mother, farewell! And if I fall, mourn not, but glory that I died as best became the son of Cleon [*draws his sword*]. And now leap forth, my sword!—henceforth is there no rest nor honor till we have conquered. Father, I come, I come! [Ion *rushes out;* Iantha *rushes to the window, tears off her veil and waves it to* Ion.]

CURTAIN

[*Tent of* Mohammed; *maps and arms lying about.* Mohammed *and* Hafiz.]

Moh'd. And spake they no word of ransom or of hostage?

Hafiz. None, sire. The lady lay as one struck dead; and the priest, foul Christian dog, bade me go hence, and tarry not.

Moh'd. And held you no speech with those about the princess. Sure, there were some to listen to thy master's word.

Hafiz. Great master, I sought in vain to set before them the royal will. At first it were as though a spell had fallen on them. Nay, some did turn aside and weep, rending their hair, as though all hope were lost. Then, when I strove to win them to some counsel, they woke to such an uproar, cursing thy perfidy, and vowing most dire and speedy vengeance on thee, clashing their weapons and crying, "Down with the pagan dogs!" Then, drawing forth their lances with fierce oaths, they drove me from the gates in such warlike manner, I could but strive with haste to make good mine escape, and without rest have I journeyed hither to bring thee tidings.

Moh'd. By the prophet! and is it thus they serve the royal messenger. But they shall rue it dearly. Cleon shall die. To-morrow's sun shall never shine for him. The proud Greeks shall learn to dread Mohammed's ire, and bend their haughty heads before him in the dust. I offer ransom, and they will not harken. I send them honorable terms, and they thrust my messenger rudely from their gates. They have dared to brave me,—they shall feel my power!

Hafiz. Mighty Mohammed, if thy poor slave might offer counsel, were it not wise to tarry till the Greeks on cooler thought shall seek thee with some treaty which may avail thee better than such hasty vengeance. How much more worthy were a heavy ransom than the life of a single miserable prince.

Moh'd. Peace, slave! I have said Cleon shall die, and, by Allah! so I have not word from these rebel dogs ere three days shall wear away, his body swung from the battlements shall bear them tidings of

Mohammed's power. [*Enter* Selim.] What hath befallen, Selim, that thou comest in such haste?

Selim. Most mighty king, there waits without a youth, demanding speech of thee.

Moh'd. A youth! Who may he be, and what seeks he with us?

Selim. Most gracious sire, I know not. Our guard surprised him wandering without the camp,—alone, unarmed, save with a single sword; young, and I think a Greek. Abdallah seized him as a spy, and led him hither to await thy royal will. He doth refuse all question, demanding to be led before thee, where he will unfold his errand.

Moh'd. A Greek! Bring him before us, an he prove a spy he shall hang before the day waxeth older by an hour. Hence,—bring him hither! [*Exit* Selim.] By Allah! my proud foes have deigned to send us messengers, and seek to win the favor so rudely scorned. They know not Mohammed, and, so they humble not themselves, will sue in vain.

[*Enter* Selim, *dragging* Ion.

Selim. Your Mightiness doth behold the youth. [*To* Ion, *who stands proudly*.] Kneel, slave!

Ion. I kneel not unto tyrants.

Moh'd. How, bold stripling! Weigh with more care thy speech, and forget not before whom thou dost stand. [*To* Selim.] Go, slave, and stand without; see that none enter here unbidden. [*Exit* Selim.] Speak, boy! Who art thou, and why dost thou seek thus fearlessly the presence of thy foe?—and beware thou speakest truly if it is as a friend to treat in honorable fashion, or as a spy, thou now standest before us.

Ion. I am a Greek, son to the noble Cleon, now thy captive; I seek his rescue.

Moh'd. Son to Cleon! Now, by the Prophet, 'tis wondrous strange! And thou hast ventured alone into the camp amid thy deadly foes? Speak, boy,—thine errand!

Ion. To offer hostage; to treat with Mohammed for a father's life; to move to pity or to justice the heart that hath doomed a noble soldier unto an unjust death.

Moh'd. And where, my bold prince, are thy followers, thy slaves, thy royal train?

Ion. On yonder plain, cold in their graves.

Moh'd. Hast thou brought ransom? Where is thy gold?

Ion. In the coffers of the Turkish Mohammed, plundered from his slaughtered foes.

Moh'd. Thou spakest of hostage,—I see it not.

Ion. 'Tis here,—the son of Cleon.

Moh'd. Thou! and thinkest thou thy young, worthless life were a fit hostage for the leader of a rebel band, the enemy of all true followers, whose capture hath cost blood and slaves and gold? By Allah! boy, thou must name a higher price to win the life thou doth seek.

Ion. I have nought else to offer. Thy hand hath rent from me friends, followers, gold, a sire. But if this young life hath any worth to thee, if these arms may toil for thee, this form bear burdens to thy royalty, take them,—take all, O king, but render unto me that life without which Greece is lost.

Moh'd. Peace! Thy speech is vain; thy life is nought to me.

Ion. I will serve thee as a slave; in all things do thy bidding,— faithful, unwearied, unrepining. Grant but my boon, and monarch shall never have a truer vassal than I will be to thee. Great Mohammed, let me not plead in vain.

Moh'd. Peace, I say; anger me not.

Ion. O king, hast thou no heart? Think of the ruined home, the mourning people, the land made desolate by thee; of her who now counts the weary hours for tidings of those dear to her,—tidings fraught with life or death as thou shalt decree; of the son by thee doomed to see his honored sire, hero of a hundred battles dragged like a slave unto a shameful death. As thou wilt have mercy shown to thee, that mercy show thou unto me. Oh, say to me, "Thy father lives!"

Moh'd. Away! I will not listen.

Ion. Nay, I *will* kneel to thee. I who never knelt to man before, now implore thee with earnest supplication. 'Tis for a father's life.

Moh'd. Kneel not to me,—it is in vain. Thy father is my captive, my deadliest foe, whom I hate, and curse,—ay, and will slay. Boy, dost thou know to whom thou dost bow?

Ion [*rising proudly*]. To the pagan Mohammed,—he who with murderous hand hath bathed in blood the smiling plains of Greece; profaned her altars, enslaved her people, and filled the land with widows' tears and orphans' cries; he who by perfidy makes captives of his foes, refusing hostage and scorning honorable treaty; turns from all suppliants, closes his heart to mercy, and tramples under foot all pity and all justice,—the murderer, and the tyrant. Yes, king, I know to whom I plead.

Moh'd. [*in great anger*]. Ho, without there, guards!—Selim! [*Enter Selim and soldiers.*] Away with the prisoner! Bind him fast; see he escape not. Mohammed stands not to be braved by a beardless boy! Hence! [*Guards approach with chains.*]

Ion. Lay not hands upon me,—I am no slave! One more appeal: May a son look once more upon his father ere death parts them forever? May I but for an hour speak with Cleon?

Moh'd. Once more thou mayst look upon the rebel Greek. When he hangs from yonder battlement thou mayst gaze unbidden as thou will. Away! With to-morrow's sun, he dies.

Ion. So soon, O king!—nay, the son of Cleon kneels not to thee again [*turns to go*].

Moh'd. Stay,—yield up thy sword! Bend thy proud knee, and surrender unto me the arms thou art unworthy now to bear.

Ion [*drawing his sword*]. This, my sword, girded on by a mother's hand, pledged to the deliverance of a captive sire, dedicated to the service of my country, unstained, unconquered,—*thus* do I surrender thee. [*He breaks the sword, and flings it down.*]

Moh'd. Again dost thou brave me! Away with the rebel! Bind him hand and foot. He shall learn what it is to be Mohammed's slave. Hence, I say!

Ion. I am thy captive, but thy slave—never! Thou mayst chain my limbs, thou canst *not* bind my freeborn soul! Lead on,—I follow.

[*Exit* Ion *and guards*.

CURTAIN

SCENE THIRD

[*Tent of* Zuleika; *guitar, ottoman, etc.*]

Zuleika [*pacing up and down*]. Night draweth on apace, and ever nearer comes the fatal hour. With to-morrow's dawn all hope is o'er, for Mohammed hath sworn the Greek shall die, and when was *he* ere known to fail in his dread purpose? In vain have I wept before him, imploring him to have some mercy; in vain have I sought with golden promises to move the stony-hearted Hafiz,—all, all hath failed, and I am in despair. And that brave youth, his true heart filled with love's pure devotion, seeking by the sacrifice of his own life to save a father! And now each moment bringeth nearer the death-hour of that father, and he is mourning in solitude that he may not say farewell. Where can I turn for help? Ah, Hassan! my faithful slave. He is true, and loveth me like his own. He must aid me [*claps her hands; enter* Hassan]. Hassan, thou lovest me, and would not see me grieve?

Hassan. Allah, forbid! Thou art dear to old Hassan as the breath of life, and while life lingers he will serve thee.

Zuleika. Then must thou aid me in a deed of mercy. Who doth keep watch to-night before the tent of the young Greek?

Hassan. Mine is the watch. Wherefore dost thou seek to know?

Zuleika. Hassan, thou hast sworn to serve me. I have a boon to ask of thee.

Hassan. Speak, lady! thy slave doth listen.

Zuleika. Thou knowest that with the morning sun Mohammed hath sworn Cleon shall die. Such is the fierce anger he doth bear his foe he hath refused all mercy and scorned to listen to the prayers of the young prince who hath journeyed hither at peril of his own life to place himself in the power of the king as hostage for his father.

Hassan. It is indeed most true. Poor youth!

Zuleika. 'Tis of him I would speak to thee. Mohammed, angered at his boldness, hath, as thou knowest, guarded him in yonder tent,

104

denying him his last sad prayer to speak once more in life with his father. Oh, Hassan, what must be the agony of that young heart to see the hours swift speeding by, and know no hope.

Hassan. What wouldst thou have me do?

Zuleika. Lead him to his father; give him the consolation of folding to his breast the beloved one to save whose life he hath sacrificed his own.

Hassan. Dear mistress, thou art dreaming, and cannot know the danger of so rash a deed. Bethink thee of Mohammed's anger, the almost certain doom of such as dare to brave his mighty will. I pray thee let not thy noble heart lead thee astray. Thou canst not save him, and will but harm thyself.

Zuleika. Hassan, thy love and true devotion, I well know, doth prompt thee to thus counsel, and in thy fear for me thou dost forget to think of mercy or of pity. I thank thee; but thou canst not move me from my firm resolve. Again I ask thee, Wilt thou aid me?

Hassan [*falling at her feet*]. Pardon, but I cannot. Heed, I implore thee, the counsel of thy faithful servant, and trust to the wisdom these gray hairs have brought. Thou art young and brave, but believe me, maiden, dangers of which thou dost not dream beset the path, and I were no true friend did I not warn thee to beware. Do not tempt me; I cannot aid thee to thy ruin.

Zuleika. Then will I go alone. I will brave the peril, and carry comfort to a suffering soul [*turns to go*; Hassan *catches her robe*].

Hassan. Maiden! once more let thy slave entreat. Thy father places faith in me. I am the captive's guard.

Zuleika. Peace, Hassan, peace; if life be then so dear to thee, and thy duty to thy king greater than that thou dost owe to thy fellow-man, Allah forbid that I should tempt thee to forget it. But did death look me in the face, I would not tarry now.

Hassan. And thou wouldst seek the captive's cell?

Zuleika. This very hour. Soon it will be too late.

Hassan. Thou knowest not the way,—soldiers guard every turn. Oh, tarry till the dawn, I do implore thee.

Zuleika. The darkness shall be my guide, Allah my guard; shrouded in yon dark mantle none will deem me other than a slave. Again I ask thee, Wilt thou go?

Hassan. I go. I were no true man to tremble when a woman fears not. I will guide thee, and may Allah in his mercy shield us both. Say thy prayers, Hassan, for thy head no longer rests in safety.

Zuleika. Come, let us on! The moments speed. The darkening gloom befriends us. First to the tent of the young prince, and while I in brief speech do acquaint him with mine errand, thou shalt keep guard without. Then will we guide him to his father, and unto Allah leave the rest [*shrouds herself in dark mantle and veil*]. Lead on, good Hassan. Let us away!

Hassan. Fold thy veil closer, that none may know the daughter of Mohammed walks thus late abroad. Come, and Allah grant we sleep not in paradise to-morrow!

[*Exit, leading* Zuleika.

CURTAIN

[Ion's *tent.* Ion *chained, in an attitude of deep despair, upon a miserable couch. He does not see the entrance of* Zuleika *and* Hassan.]

Zuleika. Stand thou without as watch, good Hassan, and warn me if any shall approach. [*Exit* Hassan.] Young Greek, despair not; hope is nigh.

Ion [*starting up*]. Bright vision, whence comest thou? Art thou the phantom of a dream, or some blest visitant from that better land, come to bear me hence? What art thou?

Zuleika. I am no vision, but a mortal maiden, come to bring thee consolation.

Ion. Consolation! ah, then indeed thou art no mortal; for unto grief like mine there is no consolation, save that which cometh from above.

Zuleika. Nay, believe it not. Human hearts are at this moment hoping, and human hands are striving earnestly to spare thee the agony thou dost dread.

Ion. Are there then hearts to feel for the poor Greek? I had thought I was alone,—alone 'mid mine enemies. Sure, those fetters are no dream, this dark cell, the words "Thy father dies!" No, no! it is a dread reality. The words are burned into my brain.

Zuleika. Is death, then, so dread a thing unto a warrior? I had thought it brought him fame and glory.

Ion. Death! Oh, maiden! To the soldier on the battle-field, fighting for his father-land 'mid the clash of arms, the fierce blows of foemen, the shouts of victory; 'neath the banner of his country, the gratitude of a nation, the glory of a hero round his brow,—death were a happy, ay, a welcome friend. But alone, 'mid foes, disgraced by fetters, dragged to a dishonored grave, with none to whisper of hope or comfort, death is a cruel, a most bitter foe.

Zuleika. Mine errand is to take from that death the bitterness thou dost mourn, to give a parting joy to the life now passing.

Ion. Oh, hast thou the power to save my father's life! Oh, use it now, and Greece shall bless thee for thy mercy!

Zuleika. Oh, that the power *were* mine, how gladly would I use it in a cause so glorious! I am but a woman, and tho' the heart is strong, the arm is very weak. I cannot save thy father, but trust I may still cheer the parting hours with a brief happiness.

Ion. Lady, thy words of kindly sympathy fall like sweet music on my troubled heart, and at thy magic call hope springeth up anew. Thou art unknown, and yet there is that within that doth whisper I may trust thee.

Zuleika. Thou mayst indeed. Heaven were not more true than I will be unto my word. [Hassan *pauses before the door*.]

Hassan. Lady, the hours are fleeting. It were best to make good speed.

Zuleika. Hassan, thou dost counsel aright; morn must not find me here. [*To* Ion.] Young Greek, thou knowest with the coming dawn thy father dies.

Ion. Ay, ere another moon doth rise that life, so dear to Greece, shall be no more; the heart that beat so nobly at his country's call be still forever,—I know it well!

Zuleika. And hast thou no last word for him, no parting wish?

Ion. O maiden, my life were a glad sacrifice, so that I might for a single hour look on him,—for the last time say, "My father, bless thy Ion."

Zuleika. That hour shall be thine. Fold thyself in yonder cloak, and follow me.

Ion. Follow thee,—and whither?

Zuleika. To thy father's presence. Thou shalt spend with him the last hours of his earthly life. Stay not; this friendly gloom will ere long pass away.

Ion [*falling on his knees and catching her robe*]. Art thou my guardian angel? Oh, may the consolation thou hath poured into a suffering soul, fall like heaven's dew upon thine own; and if the prayers of a grateful heart bring hope and joy and peace, thy life shall bloom with choicest blessings. O maiden, how do I bless thee! [*Kisses her robe.*]

Zuleika. Speak not of that,—kneel not to me, a mortal maiden. Thy gratitude is my best reward. Hassan, lead on!

Hassan. Lady, I do thy bidding. First let me lead thee to a place of safety.

Zuleika. Nay, Hassan, I tarry here,—thou canst return; I will await thee. Now make all speed,—away!

Ion. Let us hence; my heart can ill contain its joy. Oh, my father, shall I see thee, hear thy voice, feel thine arms once more about me, and die with thy blessing on my head. Heaven hath blessed my mission.

Zuleika. Shall we depart? The hour wanes.

Ion. I will follow whither thou shalt lead. But, stay! is there no danger unto thee? Will thy deed of mercy bring suffering to thee, my kind deliverer?

Zuleika. Fear not for me. Yet one pledge must I ask of thee on which my safety doth depend. 'Tis this: Swear that from the moment thou dost leave me until thou art again a prisoner here, though the path lie plain before thee thou wilt not fly.

Ion. I swear. Thou mayst trust me.

Zuleika. Yet once again. Breathe not to mortal ear the *means* by which thou sought'st thy sire, and let the memory of this hour fade from thy heart forever. [Ion *bows assent.*] What pledge have I of thy secrecy, and of thy truth?

Ion. The word of a Greek is sacred, and were not my gratitude my surest pledge to *thee*?

Zuleika. Pardon, I do trust. Now haste thee.

Ion [*pointing to his fetters*]. Thou dost forget I am a prisoner still.

Zuleika. Hassan, unloose these fetters, and give the Greek his freedom. [Hassan *takes off the chains*; Ion *springs joyfully forward.*]

Ion. Now am I free again, and with the Turk's base fetters have I cast off my fears and my despair. Hope smiles upon me, and my father calls. Oh, let us tarry not.

Zuleika [*folding a dark mantle round him*]. Thus shrouded, in safety thou mayst reach his cell; this ring will spare thee question. Hassan will guide thee, and I—will pray for thy success. Farewell! May Allah aid thee!

Ion. Lady, though I may never know thee, never look on thee again, the memory of this brief hour will never fade. The blessed gift of mercy thou dost bestow will I ever treasure with the deepest gratitude, and my fervent prayer that all Heaven's blessings may rest upon thee cease but with my life [*falls on his knee and kisses her hand*]. Pardon,—'tis my only thanks. Spirit of mercy, farewell! farewell! [*Follows* Hassan; Zuleika *gazes after him, then sinks down weeping.*]

CURTAIN

SCENE FIFTH

[*Tent of* Cleon *the Greek.* Cleon, *chained, pacing to and fro.*]

Cleon. A few short hours and all is o'er,—Cleon sleeps with his fathers. I could have wished to die like a hero in my harness, and have known my grave were watered by my loved one's tears; to take my wife once more unto my bosom; once more bless my noble Ion; and pass hence with the blest consciousness of victory won. 'Tis bitter thus to die, ingloriously and alone. [*Proudly raising his head.*] But the name of Cleon is too dear unto his people e'er to be forgotten. The memory that he strove ever for his country's welfare shall strew with tearful blessings his unhonored grave. [*Steps approach; voices are heard.*] Ah, they come! They shall find me ready. [*Enter* Ion.] Has mine hour come? I am here.

[Ion *casts off his cloak, and springs forward.*]

Ion. Father! O my father!

Cleon [*starting back wildly*]. Thou? Here!

Ion. Yes, thy Ion; bless me, Father [*kneels*].

Cleon [*raising and clasping* Ion *to his breast*]. Here, on my heart, dear one. I turn to meet my executioners, and see thee, my boy. Great Heaven, I bless thee! [*They embrace tenderly and weep.*] Thou camest thither—how?

Ion. Alone, with my good sword.

Cleon. Thy guide through the perils of the way, my child?

Ion. The good Father who doth guide all who trust in him.

Cleon. And thine errand?

Ion. To behold thee, my father, and with my life to strive for thy release.

Cleon. My noble boy, thou hast come unto thy death. Oh, who could bid thee thus brave the doom that must await thee?

111

Ion. My mother bid me forth; and as she girded on my sword, she bid me seek my father, with her blessing on my mission.

Cleon. My brave Iantha, thus for thy country's sake to doom thine own heart to so deep a sorrow [*looks sadly upon* Ion]. Tell me, my son, did thy mother bear bravely up against the fatal tidings? I had feared her tender heart might but ill meet a blow so fearful. Speak to me of her.

Ion. When the rude Turk did in rough speech acquaint her with thy fell defeat, she sank as one o'erpowered by her grief, praying the friendly hand of death might take her hence; but soon the spirit of the Greek rose high within her, and, banishing her fears, with brave and trusting heart she sent me forth to seek, and if it might be, save thee. Ah, my father, that I might die for thee!

Cleon. And thou hath come to see me die! Dost thou not know that with the night thy father passeth hence, and when the stars again look forth it will be upon his grave?

Ion. Father, 'tis because thou art doomed that I am here. And if my heart speak truly, those same bright stars shall serve to guide thee back to freedom.

Cleon. Thou doth speak wildly. What wilt thou do? Wilt *thou* brave the king?

Ion [*proudly*]. Nay, I have knelt for the last time unto Mohammed. I have offered him my liberty, my service, ay, my life itself, and he hath scorned me. I have deigned to bow before him as a suppliant, and he hath spurned me; I have sought by all the power love and despair could teach to move him, and his ear was closed to me. I seek him not again.

Cleon. Child, what hath led thee to the presence of the king? How didst thou brave the frown of him before whom even armed men do tremble? Didst thou dream thy feeble voice could reach a heart so cruel, that thy prayers could soften one who knoweth not the name of mercy?

Ion. Love can brave all dangers. It giveth wisdom to the untaught, strength to the weak, hope to the despairing, comfort to the mourner. Love hath been my guide, my guard.

Cleon. My boy! my Ion! Truly doth God place in the pure heart of such as thou his truest wisdom, his deepest faith [*embraces him*

112

with deep emotion]. But—art not thou in danger? Did not thy bold speech anger the proud king? Art thou still free?

Ion. Let not thy heart be vexed with fears for me,—I am unharmed.

Cleon. Ion, deceive me not, but as thou hopest for thy father's love, speak truly. Art thou in danger from the Turk, and in thy devotion to thy father dost thou seek to be thyself the sacrifice? Answer me, Ion.

Ion. Father, I sought to spare thy too o'erburdened heart another grief. I *am* a prisoner in Mohammed's power, and know not if my fate be life or death.

Cleon. 'Tis as I feared; and thou, the last hope of thy country, must fall,—all, all, for me! Oh, mine own disgrace were bitter, but to see thee die! Oh, woe is me!

Ion. Father, were it not better thus to die, than in disgraceful peace to pass away with no thought for our fatherland, no proud consciousness of having at the call of duty sacrificed all we held most dear, and leave a name held sacred as one who yielded life and liberty on the altar of his country?

Cleon. But that thou in thine innocence and bloom should meet death at the hands of heartless foemen; and for *my* sake! 'Tis this that tears my heart.

Ion. The purer the victim the more acceptable the sacrifice. But fear not, dear father. The Turk is yet a man; 'tis 'gainst thee he wars, and he will not wreak his vengeance on a child. He may relent, and for my love's sake, pardon mine offence.

Cleon. Child, thou knowest not Mohammed. He pardons none; all fall before him, with relentless hand,—all strew his pathway unto victory. Will he then spare and pity thee? Nay, sire and son must fall! [*Stands sorrowfully. Ion suddenly sees Zuleika's ring upon his hand, and springs forward.*]

Ion. Father, thou shalt yet breathe the air of freedom, shall clasp my mother to thy heart; once more shall lead thy gallant band onward to victory.

Cleon. Raise not bright hopes to crush them at their birth; wake not to dreams of triumph the heart that hath striven to drive hence all save the solemn thoughts meet for one so soon to pass away.

113

Ion [*pointing to the door*]. See, the gray morning 'gins to glimmer in the east. 'Tis no time for despair. Haste, Father, freedom is near!

Cleon. What doth thus move thee, Ion? Dost thou forget these chains, the guards, the perils at each step? Thou art dreaming!

Ion. I tell thee 'tis no dream. Thou shalt be free. This mantle will disguise thee; this ring open a pathway through the guards; these stars shall be thy silent guide. Wilt thou go?

Cleon. 'Tis strange! Whence then that ring? How dost thou, a captive, wander thus freely, and offer liberty with such a bounteous hand?

Ion. A solemn oath doth forbid me to reveal to living man the secret of this hour; but if ever angels do leave their homes to minister to suffering souls, 'twas one most bright and beautiful who hath this night led me unto thee, and placed in mine hand the power to set thee free.

Cleon. Truth speaketh in thine earnest eye and pleading voice, and yet I dare not listen to thy tale.

Ion. Oh, Father, heed not thy fears, thy doubts! Take thy liberty, believing it heaven-sent. No oath binds thee to Mohammed; thou art no rightful prisoner of war,—neither duty nor honor doth demand thy stay. Thy country calls, and Heaven doth point the way.

Cleon. 'Tis true; no oath doth bind me to the Turk, and yet to fly— My soldier's spirit doth ill brook such retreat.

Ion. Then stay not, my father, but whilst thou may, depart.

Cleon. Bright hopes call me hence. Life, love, fame, beckon me away.

[Hassan *looks in.*]

Hassan. The promised hour hath well-nigh gone. Prepare, young Greek; we must away.

Ion. A moment more. [*Exit* Hassan.] Father, time wanes. Once more I do entreat thee,—go!

Cleon. Heaven grant I choose aright! Come Ion, we will forth together. [Ion *folds the cloak about* Cleon; *gives him the ring.*] Come, let us go.

Ion. Nay, but one can pass forth. Thou goest. I await the morning here.

Cleon. Then do I tarry also. Nay, Ion, I will not go hence without thee.

Ion. Then all is lost. Father, thy stay can nought avail me. It cannot save, and thou wilt but sacrifice thine own priceless life.

Cleon. Then fly with me; let me bear thee to thy mother. Alone, I will not go.

Ion. I cannot go; a vow doth bid me stay,—a vow that nought shall tempt me from the camp to-night; and when did a Greek e'er break his plighted word?

Cleon. If thine honor bid thee stay, thy father will not tempt thee hence; but he may stay and suffer with thee the fate of the faithful [*throws off the mantle*].

Ion. Oh, my father, do not cast from thee the priceless boon of liberty. Think of thy broken-hearted wife, thy faithful followers, thy unconquered foes; think, Father, of thy country calling on thee for deliverance. What were my worthless life weighed 'gainst her freedom. And what happier fate for a hero's son than for a hero's sake to fall!

Cleon. Thou true son of Greece! Mayst thou yet live to wield a sword for thine oppressed land, and gird with laurels that brow so worthy them.

[Hassan *enters*.

Hassan. No longer may I stay: thine hour is past.

Ion. I come,—yet one moment more, good Hassan; it is my last. [*Exit* Hassan.] Once more, my father, do I entreat thee,—go. Thou dost forget a guardian spirit watcheth over me, and the power that led me hither may yet accomplish my deliverance. If nought else can move thee, for my sake go, and win for me that freedom mine honor doth now forbid me to seek. Break not my heart, nor let me plead in vain.

Cleon. My boy, for thy dear sake do I consent. I *will* earn thy deliverance bravely, as a soldier should; and thy dear image shall be to me the star that leads me on to victory.

Ion [*joyfully*]. Away! Hassan will guide thee past the guards. Then fly,—and Heaven guide thee, O my father! [Ion *again shrouds* Cleon *in the mantle, concealing his chains in the thick folds*.] Thus muffle thy tell-tale fetters, that no sound may whisper to the Turks there walks a Greek under the free heavens forth to freedom.

Cleon. My Ion, one last embrace! God grant 'tis not our last on earth! Bless thee, thou true young heart! Heaven guard thee!

[Hassan *enters in haste.*

Hassan. Art ready? We must depart. [Cleon *bows his head and follows.* Ion *rushes after, looking from the tent.*]

Ion. Saved! saved! The morning sun that was to shine upon his grave, will smile upon him far, far from foemen's power. And Mohammed, thinking to look upon a dying slave, shall waken to the sound of his victorious war-trump. Ion, thy mission is accomplished. Thou hast given a saviour to thy fatherland, and mayst fall thyself without a murmur [*looks up thankfully; a loud noise without*].

[*Enter* Abdallah *and* Murad.

Abd. Where is the prisoner? Come forth!

Ion. I am here [*comes forward*].

Abd. Ha!—here is treason! Without there!—the prisoner hath escaped!

Murad. Who flieth yonder, past the camp?

Abd. 'Tis he! Forth, call for aid! Search without delay! Here is foul work abroad. First, seize yon boy; fetter the base spy; bear him before the king. Speed hence!

Murad [*to* Ion]. Infidel dog, thou shalt learn what it is to brave Mohammed's ire!

[*They seize* Ion, *and drag him away.*]

CURTAIN

BIANCA

OPERATIC TRAGEDY

NOTE TO BIANCA

The peculiarity of this opera was that while the words were committed to memory, the music was *composed* and *sung* as the scene proceeded.

In spite of its absurdity, this play was a great favorite; for Jo was truly superb as the hapless Bianca, while her trills and tragic agonies were considered worthy of the famous Grisi herself.

CHARACTERS

Adelbert *Betrothed to Bianca.*

Huon *His Rival.*

Juan *A Page.*

Bianca *A Spanish Lady.*

Hilda *A Witch.*

SCENE FIRST

[*A wood. Enter* Huon.]

Huon. Hist! All is still. They are not yet here. On this spot will the happy lovers meet. O wretched Huon! she whom thou so passionately doth love will here speak tender words to thy thrice hated rival. Yet I, unseen, will watch them, and ere long my fierce revenge shall change their joy to deepest woe. Hark! they come! Now, jealous heart, be still! [*Hides among the trees.*]

[*Enter* Bianca *and* Adelbert.

Adel. Nay, dearest love, fear not; no mortal eye beholds us now, and yon bright moon looks kindly down upon our love.

[*They seat themselves beneath the trees.*

Bianca. Ah, dearest Adelbert, with thee I feel no fear, but thy fierce rival Huon did vow vengeance on thee, for I did reject his suit for thine. Beware! for his wild heart can feel no pity, tenderness, or love.

Adel. I fear him not. Ere long thou wilt be mine, and then in our fair home we will forget all but our love. Think not, dearest, of that dark, revengeful man; he does not truly love thee.

Bianca. Near thee I cannot fear; but when thou art far from me, my fond heart will ever dread some danger for thee. Ah, see the moon is waning; dear love, thou must away.

Adel. Ah, sweet moments, why so quickly fled? 'Tis hard to leave thee, thou bright star in my life's sky, and yet I must, or all may be betrayed. Fare thee well, dear love. One sweet kiss ere we part! [*They embrace.*]

Bianca. Farewell! Ah, when shall I again behold thee? Oh, be not long away, for like a caged bird I pine for thee.

Adel. When next yon moon doth rise beneath thy lattice, thou shalt hear my light guitar.

Bianca. Fail not to come. I shall watch for thee the live-long night, and if thou comest not, this fond heart will grieve.

Both. Farewell, till yon bright moon doth rise,
Farewell, dear love, farewell!
Farewell, farewell, farewell!
Farewell, dear love, farewell!

[*Exit* Adelbert.

Bianca. Ah, love, thou magic power, thus ever make my breast thy home. Adieu, dear spot! I fly to happiness and—

Huon. *Me*—[Bianca *shrieks, and seeks to fly*. Huon *detains her.*]

Bianca. Unmanly villain, touch me not. What dost thou here concealed?

Huon. I listen to thy lover's fond and heartless vows. What is his love to mine? Ah, lady, he loves thee for thy wealth alone. Again I ask, nay, I implore thee to be mine! Oh, grant me now my prayer!

Bianca. Never! never! I will not listen to thee more. My heart is all another's; my hatred and contempt are thine.

[*Exit* Bianca.

Huon. Now, by yon moon 'neath which thy tender vows were plighted, do I swear to win thee, proud and haughty lady, to these arms. Thou shalt curse the day when thou didst cast away my love, and wake my deep revenge.

[*Exit* Huon.

CURTAIN

SCENE SECOND

[*A cave in the forest.* Hilda *leaning over a boiling caldron. Enter* Huon.]

Hilda. Ha! who art thou, and what wouldst thou with old Hilda? Speak, and be obeyed.

Huon. O mighty wizard, I have sought thee for a charm to win a proud and scornful woman's love,—some mystic potion that shall make her cold heart burn for me. Ah, give me this, and gold uncounted shall be thine.

Hilda. I will give to thee a draught that shall chase her coldness and her pride away, and make the heart now beating for another all thine own. Hold! 'tis here,—three crimson drops when mingled in her wine, will bring the boon thou askest [*gives* Huon *a tiny phial*].

Huon. Oh, blessed draught that wins for me the love I seek. Proud Bianca, now art thou in my power, and shalt ere long return the love of the once hated and despised Huon. Great sorceress, say how can I repay thee? Fear not to claim thy just reward.

Hilda. I ask no gold. But when thy prize is won, remember thou old Hilda's warning. Woman's heart is a fragile thing, and they who trifle with it should beware. Now go; I would be alone.

Huon. Farewell! When my love and my revenge are won, I'll bless this hour and Hilda's charm.

[*Exit* Huon.

Hilda. Poor fool! thou little thinkest thy love-charm is a deadly draught, and they who quaff it die. When thou shalt seek thy lady, hoping for her love, a dead bride thou wilt win. Ha! ha! old Hilda's spells work silently and well.

CURTAIN

SCENE THIRD

[*Room in the castle of* Bianca. *Evening. Enter* Huon.]

Huon. How can I best give the draught that none may see the deed? Ha! yonder comes her page, bearing wine. Now in her cup will I mingle these enchanted drops, and she shall smile on me when next I plead my suit. Ho, Juan, my boy! come hither; I would speak with thee. [*Enter* Juan *with wine.*] Where is thy lady now?

Juan. At her lattice, watching for Lord Adelbert, and gazing on the flowers he hath sent.

Huon [*aside*]. She shall never watch and wait for him again. [*Aloud.*] Whence bearest thou the wine, Juan? Is it to thy lady?

Juan. Yes, my lord. She bid me haste. I must away.

Huon. Stay! clasp my sandal, boy; I will repay thee if thy mistress chide. [Juan *stoops;* Huon *drops the potion into the wine cup.*] Thanks; here is gold for thee. Away, and tell thy lady I will be here anon.

[*Exit* Juan.

Ha, ha! 'tis done! 'tis done!
My vengeance now is won,
And ere to-morrow's sun shall set,
Thou, haughty lady, shalt forget
The lover who now hastes to thee,
And smile alone, alone on me.

[*Exit* Huon.

CURTAIN

SCENE FOURTH

[Bianca's *castle. A moonlit balcony. Enter* Bianca.]

Bianca. He comes not. Yon bright moon will ere long set, and still I hear not the dear voice 'neath my lattice singing. Adelbert! Ah, come! Hist! I hear his light boat on the lake. 'Tis he! 'tis he! [*Leans over the balcony.*]

[Adelbert *sings in the garden below.*

The moon is up, wake, lady, wake!
My bark is moored on yonder lake.
The stars' soft eyes alone can see
My meeting, dear one, here with thee.

Wake, dearest, wake! lean from thy bower,
The moonlight gleams on tree and flower.
The summer sky smiles soft above;
Look down on me, thou star of love!

Bianca. Adelbert, dear love, now haste thee quickly up to me.

[*Enter* Adelbert *upon the balcony.*

Adel. Sweet love, why fearest thou? None dare stay me when I fly to thee. Ah, sit thee here, and I will rest beside thee. [Bianca *seats herself;* Adelbert *lies at her feet.*]

Bianca. Thou art weary, love. I'll bring thee wine, and thou shalt rest while I do sing to thee. [*She gives him wine; he drinks.*]

Adel. Thanks to thee, dearest love, I am weary now no longer. When here beside thee, pain, sorrow, time are all forgot. Ah! what is this?—a deadly pang hath seized me. All grows dark before mine eyes. I cannot see thee. Yon cup,—'twas poisoned! I am dying, dying!

Bianca. Ah, nay, thou art faint! Speak not of dying, love. [Adelbert *falls.*] Adelbert, Adelbert, speak!—speak! It is thine own Bianca calls thee! [*Throws herself beside him.*]

122

Adel. Farewell, dear love, farewell! Huon hath won his vengeance now. God bless thee, dearest. Oh, farewell! [*Dies.*]

Bianca. Awake! awake! All, cold and still! Thou true, brave heart, thou art hushed forever. Huon! yes! 'twas he; and he hath sought to win me thus. But 'tis in vain! Where is the poisoned cup that I may join thee, Adelbert? [*Takes the cup.*] Ah, 'tis gone: there is no more. Yet I will be with thee, my murdered love. For me life hath no joy, and I will find thee even in death [*falls fainting to the ground*].

CURTAIN

SCENE FIFTH

[Bianca's *castle. The garden.* Bianca *singing.*]

Faded flowers, faded flowers,
They are all now left to cherish;
For the hopes and joys of my young life's spring
I have seen so darkly perish.

Cold, ah, cold, in the lone, dark grave,
My murdered love lies low,
And death alone can bring sure rest
To this broken heart's deep woe.

Faded flowers, faded flowers,
They are all now left to cherish;
For ah, his dear hand gathered them,
And my love can never perish.

[*Weeps.*

[*Enter* Huon *and kneels at her feet.*

Bianca [*starting up*]. Fiend! demon! touch me not with hands that murdered him! Hence! out of my sight,—away!

Huon. Nay, lady, nay! I swear by Heaven it was not I. The spell I mingled in thy cup was but to win thy love. The old witch hath deceived me, and given that deadly poison. Forgive me, I implore thee, and here let me offer thee my love once more.

Bianca [*repulsing him*]. *Love!* darest thou to speak of love to me, whose bright dream of life thou hast destroyed? *Love!* I who loathe, scorn, hate thee with a deep and burning hate that death alone can still! Oh, Heaven, have mercy on my tortured heart, and let it break.

Huon [*aside*]. His death hath well-nigh driven her mad. Dear lady, grieve not thus. Let me console thee. Forget thy love, and seek in mine the joy thou hast lost.

Bianca. Forget! Ah, never, never, till in death I join him! Forgive thee? Not till I have told thy crime. Yes, think not I will rest till thou,

124

my murdered Adelbert, art well avenged. And thou!—ah, sinful man, tremble, for thou art in my power, and my wronged heart can feel no pity now.

Huon [*fiercely*]. Wouldst thou betray me? Never! Yield thou to my love, or I will sheathe my dagger in thy heart, and silence thee forever!

Bianca. I will not yield. The world shall know thy guilt, and then sweet death shall be a blessing.

Huon. Then die, and free me from the love and fear that hang like clouds above me [*stabs her*].

Bianca. Thy sin will yet be known, and may God pardon thee! O earth, farewell! My Adelbert, I come, I come! [*Dies.*]

Huon. Dead! dead! Oh, wretched Huon! Where now seek rest from bitter memories and remorse. Ha, a step! I must fly. Angel, fare thee well!

[*Exit* Huon.

CURTAIN

SCENE SIXTH

[Huon's *room*. Huon *asleep upon a couch. Enter* Bianca's *spirit. She lays her hand upon him.*]

Huon [*starting in affright*]. Ha! spirit of the dead, what wouldst thou now? For long, long nights why hast thou haunted me? Cannot my agony, remorse, and tears win thee to forget? Ah, touch me not! Away! away! See how the vision follows. It holds me fast. Bianca, save me! save me! [*Falls and dies.*]

[*Tableau.*

CURTAIN

THE UNLOVED WIFE;

OR,

WOMAN'S FAITH

CHARACTERS

Count Adrian *Nina's Husband.*

Don Felix *His Secret Rival.*

Nina *The Unloved Wife.*

Hagar *A Fortune Teller.*

SCENE FIRST

[*Room in the palace of* Count Adrian. *Enter* Nina.]

Nina. 'Tis a fair and lovely home and well befits a gay young bride; but ah, not if she bear a sad and weary heart like mine beneath her bridal robes. All smile on me and call me happy, blessed with such a home and husband; and yet 'mid all my splendor I could envy the poor cottage maiden at her spinning-wheel. For ah, 'mid all her poverty one sweet thought comes ever like a sunny sky to brighten e'en her darkest hours, for she is loved; while I yet sigh in vain for one kind word, one tender glance, from him I love so fondly. Ah, he comes, no sad tears now, sorrow is for my lonely hours and I will smile on *him* e'en though my heart is breaking.

[*Enter* Count Adrian.

Adrian [*coldly*]. Good-even, madam, I trust all things are placed befitting a fair lady's bower and thou hast found thy home a pleasant one.

Nina. Adrian, husband, speak not thus to me. I could find more joy in some poor cell with thee, than all the wealth that kings could give if thou wert gone. Look kindly on me and I ask no more. One smile from thee can brighten all the world to these fond eyes. Oh, turn not away, but tell me how have I angered thee, and grant thy pardon for thy young wife's first offence.

Adrian. The pardon I could give were worthless for the time is past. 'Tis too late to ask forgiveness now. It matters not, then say no more [*turns away*].

Nina. My lord, I charge thee tell me of what dark crime thou dost think me guilty! Fear not to tell me; innocence is strong to bear and happy to forgive. Ah, leave me not, I cannot rest till I know all, and if the deep devotion of a woman's heart can still repair the wrong, it shall be thine—but answer me.

Adrian. Canst thou unsay the solemn words that bound us at the altar three short days ago? Canst thou give back the freedom thou hast taken, break the vows thou hast plighted, cast away that ring and tell me I am free? Do it, and my full forgiveness shall be thine.

Nina. Give thee back thy freedom; am I a chain to bind thee to what thou dost not love? Take back the vows I made to honor thee; what dost thou mean? I am thy wife and dost thou hate me?

Adrian. I do.

Nina. God help me now. Tell me, Adrian, I implore thee, tell me what have I done to tempt such cruel words from thee? I loved thee and left all to be thy wife, and now when my poor heart is longing for one tender word to cheer its sorrow, thou, the husband who hath vowed to love and cherish me, hath said thou dost hate me. Ah, am I sleeping? Wake me or the dream will drive me mad.

Adrian. 'Tis a dream I cannot banish. We must part.

Nina. Part—go on, the blow hath fallen, I can feel no more. Go on.

Adrian. Thou knowest I wooed thee. Thou wert fair and wondrous rich; I sought thy gold, not *thee*, for with thy wealth I would carve out a path through life that all should honor. Well, we were wed, and when I sought to take thy fortune it was gone, and not to me, but to thy father's friend, Don Felix. It was all left to him, and thou wert penniless; and thus I won a wife I loved not, and lost the gold I would have died to gain. Thinkest thou not I am well angered? But for thee I might yet win a noble bride whose golden fetters I would gladly wear.

Nina. And this is he to whom I gave my heart so filled with boundless love and trust. Oh, Adrian, art thou so false? What is gold to a woman's deathless love? Can it buy thee peace and all the holy feelings human hearts can give? Can it cheer and comfort thee in sorrow, or weep fond, happy tears when thou hast won the joy and honor thou dost seek? No, none of these, the golden chains will bind thee fast till no sweet thought, no tender hope can come to thee. I plead not now for my poor self, but for thine own heart thou doth wrong so cruelly by such vain dreams.

Adrian. Enough. Thou hast a noble name and men will honor thee, thou wilt suffer neither pain nor want. I will leave thee and wander forth to seek mine own sad lot. Farewell, and when they ask thee for thy husband, tell them thou hast none, and so be happy [*turns to go*].

129

Nina. Oh, Adrian, I implore thee stay. I will bear all thy coldness, ay even thy contempt. I will toil for thee and seek to win the gold for which thou dost sigh, I will serve thee well and truly, for with all my heart I love thee still. Leave me not now or I shall die! [*Kneels and clasps his hand.*]

Adrian. I am a slave till death shall set me free. We shall not meet again. Nay, kneel not to me. I do forgive thee, but I cannot love thee [*rushes out*].

Nina. This is more than I can bear. Oh, Father, take thy poor child home, and still the sorrow of this broken heart.

CURTAIN

SCENE SECOND

[*Home of* Hagar, *the gypsy. Enter* Hagar *and* Nina.]

Hagar. What brings thee hither, gentle lady, and how can the wanderer serve the high-born and the fair?

Nina [*sadly*]. There is often deeper sorrow in the palace than the cot, good Hagar, and I seek thee for some counsel that will cure the pain of a lonely heart. I have tried all others' skill in vain, and come to thee so learned in mystic lore to give me help. I am rich and can repay thee well.

Hagar. I can read a sad tale in thy pale and gentle face, dear lady. Thou art young and loving, but the hope of youth is gone; and thou art sorrowing with no fond heart whereon to lean, no tender voice to comfort and to cheer. Ah, have I read aright? Then the only charm to still thy pain is death.

Nina. 'Tis death I long for. That still, dreamless sleep would bring me peace. But 'tis a fearful thing to take the life God gave, and I dare not. Canst thou not give me help?

Hagar. Within this tiny casket there is that which brings a quiet sleep filled with happy dreams, and they who drink the draught lie down and slumber, and if not awakened it will end in death. But thou, sweet lady, wouldst not leave this fair world yet. Tell me more, for this old heart is warm and tender still, and perchance I can help thee.

Nina. 'Tis strange that I can feel such faith in thee, kind friend, but I am young and lonely and I seek some heart for counsel. Thou art from my own fair land and I will tell thee of my sorrow. 'Tis a short, sad tale. I loved, was wed, and then—oh, darksome day—I learned my husband felt no love, and sought me only for my gold. I was penniless, and thus he cast me off; and now for long, long weeks I have not seen him, for he would not dwell with her who loved him more than life itself. Now give me some sweet charm to win that lost heart back. Ah, Hagar, help me.

Hagar. I can give thee no truer charm than that fair face and noble

131

soul, dear lady. Be thou but firm and faithful in thy love and it will win thy husband back. God bless and grant all happiness to one who doth so truly need it.

Nina. Give me the casket; and when life hath grown too bitter to be borne then will I gladly lay the burden down, and blessing him I love so well sleep that calm slumber that knows no awaking. Farewell, Hagar, thou hast given me comfort and I thank thee.

[*Exit* Nina.

CURTAIN

SCENE THIRD

[*One year is supposed to have elapsed. A room in the palace of* Nina. *Enter* Adrian *disguised.*]

Adrian. Here last I saw her one long year ago. How the wild, sweet voice still rings in my ear imploring me to stay. I can find no rest save here; and thus do I seek my home, worn out by my long wandering, and trusting to learn tidings of poor Nina. If she be true and love me still I will cast away my pride, my coldness, and all vain hopes of wealth, and let the sunlight of that pure, young life brighten my life henceforth. I hear a step, and will hide here, perchance I may thus see her [*hides behind curtain*].

[*Enter* Nina.

Nina. No rest for thee poor heart, ever whispering that dear name, ever sorrowing for those hard words that gave so deep a wound. All is dark and lonely, for he is gone. Only these withered flowers, dearer by far than my most costly gems, for his hand hath touched them, and he smiled on me when they were given. Oh, Adrian, wilt thou never give one tender thought to her who still loves and prays for thee? Death will soon free thee from thy hated wife.

[*Exit* Nina.

Adrian [*stealing forth*]. And this is she, whose pure young love I have cast away, the fond, trusting bride I left alone and friendless. She still loves on, and offers up her prayers for one who sought to break that tender heart so cruelly. I will watch well and guard thee, Nina; and if thou art truly mine thou shalt find a happy home with him thy patient love hath won.

[*Exit* Adrian *and re-enter* Nina.

Nina [*with* Adrian's *picture*]. Ah, these cold eyes smile kindly on me here, and the lips seem speaking tender words. Other faces are perchance more fair, but none so dear to me. Oh, husband, thou hast cast me off; and yet, though lonely and forsaken, I still can cherish loving thoughts of thee, and round thy image gather all the tender feelings that a woman's heart can know. Thy cruel words I can forgive, and the trusting love I gave thee glows as warmly now

133

as when thou didst cast it by and left me broken-hearted [*weeps*; *enter* Don Felix]. My lord, what seekest thou with me? Thou dost smile. Ah, hast thou tidings of my husband? Tell me quickly, I beseech thee.

Don Felix. Nay, dear lady—But sit thee down and let me tell thee why I came. [*He leads her to a sofa.*] Thou knowest I have been with thee from a child. I stood beside thee at the altar, and was the first to cheer and comfort thee when thou wast left deserted and alone. Let me now ask thee, Wouldst thou not gladly change thy sad lot here for a gay and joyous life with one who loves thee fondly?

Nina. It were indeed a happy lot to be so loved and cherished; but where, alas, is he who could thus feel for one so lonely and forsaken?

Don Felix [*kneeling*]. Here at thy feet, dear Nina. Nay, do not turn away, but let me tell thee of the love that hath grown within my heart. [*Nina starts up.*] Thy wedded lord hath cast thee off. The law can free thee. Ah, then be mine, and let me win and wear the lovely flower which he hath cast away.

Nina. Lord Felix, as the wife of him thou dost so wrong, I answer thee. Dost thou not know the more a woman's heart is crushed and wounded the more tenderly it clings where first it loved; and though deserted, ay, though hated, I had rather be the slighted wife of him, than the honored bride of the false Costella. Now leave me—I would be alone.

Don Felix. A time will come, proud woman, when thou shalt bend the knee to him whom now thou dost so scorn. Beware, for I will have a fierce revenge for the proud words thou hast spoken.

Nina. I am strong in mine own heart and fear thee not. Work thy will and thou shalt find the wife of Adrian de Mortemar needs no protector save her own fearless hand.

[*Exit* Nina.

Don Felix. Now, by my faith, thou shalt bow that haughty head, and sue to me for mercy, and I will deny it. I'll win her yet, she shall not idly brave my anger. Now to my work,—revenge.

[*Exit* Don Felix.

CURTAIN

SCENE FOURTH

[*Apartment in palace of* Nina. Nina *alone.*]

Nina. Ever thus alone, mourning for him who loves me not; was ever heart so sad as mine. Oh, Adrian, couldst thou but return even for one short hour to thy poor Nina. [*Enter* Adrian, *disguised.*] Ha, who art thou that dares to enter here in such mysterious guise? Thine errand, quickly,—speak.

Adrian. Forgive me, lady, if I cause thee fear; I would have thee know me as a friend, one who will watch above thee, and seek to spare thee every sorrow. Dear lady, think me not too bold, for I have known thee long and have a right to all thy confidence. Thy husband was my nearest friend; and, when he left thee friendless and alone, I vowed to guard and save thee in all peril. Wilt thou trust me? See, I bear his ring,—thou knowest it?

Nina. 'Tis indeed his ring. Whence came it? Ah, hast thou seen him? Tell me, and I will give thee all my confidence and thanks [*takes the ring and gazes beseechingly upon* Adrian, *who turns aside*].

Adrian. He is well, lady, and happy as one can be who bears a cold, proud heart within his breast. He has cast away an angel who could have cheered and blessed his life, and sought to find in gold the happiness thy love alone could bring. He has suffered, as he well deserves to do. Spend not thy pity upon him.

Nina [*proudly*]. And who art thou to speak thus of him? Thou canst not judge till thou also hast been tried and like him deceived. He sought for wealth to bring him fame and honor; and when he found it not, what wonder that he cast aside the love that could not bring him happiness. Thou art no true friend to speak thus of one so worthy to be loved. And think not I reproach him for my lonely lot. Ah, no, I still love on; and if he wins the wealth he covets I can give my heart's best blessing, and so pass away that he shall never know whose hand hath crushed the flower that would have clung about his life and shed its perfume there [*turns away weeping*].

Adrian [*aside*]. She loves me still. I'll try her further [*aloud*]. Lady, idle tongues have whispered that when thy lord deserted thee thou

135

didst find a solace for thy grief in a new lover's smiles. Perchance yon picture may be some gay lord who hath cheered thy solitude and won thy heart. I fain would ask thee.

Nina. Sir stranger, little dost thou know a woman's heart. I have found a comfort for my lonely hours in weeping o'er the face whose smiles could brighten life for me, or dim it by disdain and coldness. The face is there; my first, last, only love is given to him who thinks it worthless and hath cast it by.

Adrian [*taking the picture*]. 'Tis the Count, thy husband. Lady, he is unworthy such true love; leave him to his fate, and let not thy life be darkened by his cruelty and hate.

Nina. Thou canst not tempt me to forget. No other love can win me from the only one who hath a place within my heart. Let me cherish all the memories of him, and till life shall cease be true unto my husband. Now leave me, unknown friend; I trust thee for his sake, and will accept thy friendship and protection. I offer thee my gratitude and thanks for thy kind service, and will gladly seek how best I may repay it.

Adrian. Thanks, lady. Thou shalt find me true and faithful, and my best reward will be the joy I labor to restore to thee [*kneels and kisses her hand*].

Nina. Farewell, again I thank thee.

[*Exit* Nina.

Adrian. So young, so lovely, so forsaken, who would not pity and protect. I will guard her well, and ere long claim the treasure I so madly cast away ere I had learned its priceless value. Nina, thou shalt yet be happy on the bosom of thy erring and repentant husband.

[*Exit* Adrian.

CURTAIN

SCENE FIFTH

[*Hall in the palace of* Nina. *Enter* Nina *and* Don Felix.]

Nina. I tell thee, my lord, I will not listen, naught thou canst say will change my firm resolve. I cannot wed thee.

Don Felix. Nay, then listen. Thy cruel husband left thee and for one long year thou hast sorrowed in thy lonely home, and would not be comforted. He hath returned.

Nina. Ah—[*Rushes forward.*]

Don Felix. Thou may'st well start, but think not he will come to thee, chains hold him fast and—mark ye—'twas *I* who bound those chains.

Nina. Do I dream, my husband here and in captivity; nay, I believe thee not. 'Tis a false tale to anger me. I heed thee not [*turns away haughtily*].

Don Felix. Thou wilt heed me ere I am done. What thinkest thou of this thy husband's dagger? See, here his name. 'Twas taken from his hands ere the cold chains bound them. Ah, thou dost believe me now!

Nina. Oh, tell on. I *will* listen now. Why hast thou done this cruel deed? Why make this his welcome home? Thou hast fettered and imprisoned him and now art here to tell me of it? Ah, dost thou hate him? Then give all thy hate to me; but oh, I pray thee, comfort him.

Don Felix. When thou didst reject my suit, I told thee I would be revenged; I said a day would come when thou, so cold and haughty then, would kneel to me imploring mercy and I would deny thee. That time hath come, and I am deaf to all thy prayers.

Nina. For his sake will I kneel to thee beseeching liberty for *him*. I had no love to give thee. Ah, pardon if I spake with scorn, and pity me. What can I do to win thee back to mercy? Ah, listen and be generous.

137

Don Felix. 'Tis now too late. He is in my power; and a dagger can soon rid thee of a cruel husband, me of a hated rival.

Nina. God have pity on me now. Don Felix, let me plead once more. Set Adrian free, and I will take his place in yon dark cell and welcome there the dagger that shall set me free.

Don Felix. And wilt *thou* wear the chains? Wilt enter that lone cell and perish there? Canst thou do this?

Nina. Ay, gladly will I suffer pain, captivity, and death, for thee, Adrian, for thee.

Don Felix. Then woman's love is stronger than man's hate, and I envy him you would die for, Nina.

Nina. Ah, love alone can make home blest, and here it dwells not. I can free him from his fetters and his hated wife. Tell him I loved him to the last, and blessed him ere I died. Lead on, my lord, I am ready.

Don Felix [*aside*]. I thought I had steeled my heart with hatred and revenge; but oh, they pass away before such holy love as this. Would I could win her to myself, for she would lead me on to virtue and to happiness. Yet one more trial and she may be mine at last.

[*Tableaux.*

CURTAIN

SCENE SIXTH

[*Street near* Adrian's *palace. Enter* Adrian.]

Adrian. 'Tis all discovered, my mysterious captivity and my release. Don Felix, whom I trusted, wove the dark plot and sought by false words to win Nina from me. He has dared to love her; and he shall dearly pay for his presumption. He knows not that I watched above her in disguise; and now while I was in captivity he hath taken her from her home. Let him beware. If aught of harm hath come to her, woe betide him who hath caused one tear to fall, or one sad fear to trouble her. I must seek and save her. No peril will be too great to win her back to this heart that longs so fondly for her now.

[*Exit* Adrian.

CURTAIN

SCENE SEVENTH

[*A cell in the palace of* Don Felix. Nina *chained.*]

Nina. 'T is strange; here in this dark cell, tho' fettered and alone, I feel a deeper joy than when a proud and envied bride I dwelt in my deserted home. For here his foot hath trod; these walls have echoed to the voice I love; these chains so cold and heavy I more gladly wear than e'en the costly gems once clasped upon these arms, for they were his. Here his sad tears fell perchance for his captivity; but I can smile and bless the hour when I could win thy freedom, Adrian, with my poor liberty. Hark—they come. Is it to claim the vow I made to yield my bosom to the dagger meant for his? I am ready. [*Enter* Don Felix.] Alone, my lord; methought it were too sad a task for thee to take my life. Well, be it so; you claim my vow. I can die still blessing thee, my Adrian [*kneels before* Don Felix].

Don Felix. Rise, Nina; ah, kneel not to me, nor think this hand could take the life it prizes more than happiness or honor. I came not here to harm thee; Heaven forbid! I came once more to offer thee my heart, my home, and all the boundless love you have so scorned. Thy husband hath deserted thee; no ties too fast to sever bind thee to him. Thou art alone, a captive, and I alone can free thee. Think of the love I bear thee, Nina, and be mine [*takes her hand*].

Nina. Where is thy boasted honor now? Where the solemn vow thou didst make me that my lonely cell should be as sacred to thee as my palace halls? Where is thy pity for the helpless wife of him whom thou didst call thy friend? I never loved thee, now I scorn thee. A true and pure affection never binds such chains as these, nor causes bitter tears like mine to flow. Rather suffer death than cherish in my heart one tender thought of thee. Thou hast my answer, now leave me.

Don Felix. Not yet, proud captive. I have sought to win thee gently; but now, beware. Think not to escape me, thou shalt feel how deep a vengeance I can bring on thee and him thou lovest. Thou shalt suffer all the sorrow I can inflict,—shalt know thy proud lord forsaken and in danger when a word from me can save, and *that* word I will not speak. All the grief and pain and hatred that my jealous heart can give will I heap upon his head, and thus through him I will revenge myself on thee.

Nina. Thou canst not harm him, he is safe and free. Do thy worst, I care not what fate thou hast for me, a fearless hand soon finds a way to free a soul from sorrow and captivity. This heart thou canst not reach. It fears thee not.

Don Felix. Can I not make thee tremble, haughty woman? I love thee still, and I will win thee. I go to work thee sorrow; and when next we meet I will bring thee token of thy husband's death or, what may touch thee nearer, his hate of thee.

[*Exit* Don Felix.

Nina. 'Tis a dark and fearful dream,—Adrian in danger, and I cannot save him. Oh, that I were free again, naught should stay me; and I would win him back by the power of woman's love and faith. Lord Felix will return, he hath vowed revenge; where then can I look for a true heart to comfort and protect me [*sinks down in despair*].

[*Enter* Adrian, *still in disguise*.

Adrian. Here is a friend to aid thee.

Nina [*starting up*]. Who—who art thou?

Adrian. Thy guardian. Lady, thou hast said thou wouldst trust me, and I am here to save.

Nina. Forgive me that I doubt thee; yet I do fear to trust, for I am well-nigh crazed with sorrow. Art thou my husband's friend?

Adrian. I am true as Heaven to thee, poor lady. I have watched above thee and can save. Here, here is the ring thou knowest; ah, do not doubt me.

Nina. I know thee now and put all my faith in thee. Take me hence. Ah, save me! Lead me to my home, and the thanks of a broken heart are thine. Lead on, kind friend, I will follow thee.

Adrian [*aside*]. Oh, this is a bitter punishment for me. It breaks my heart. [Aloud.] This way, dear lady, a secret door doth let us forth; step thou lightly. Thus let me shroud thee.

[*He wraps* Nina *in a dark robe, and they disappear thro' the secret door.*

CURTAIN

SCENE EIGHTH

[Nina's *chamber. Enter* Nina *and* Hagar.]

Nina. Welcome to thee, Hagar; sit thee down and tell me why hast thou come to seek me in my lonely home?

Hagar. Sweet lady, fear not; no evil tidings do I bring, but a wondrous tale of happiness in store for thee. When thy father died, few doubted but his wealth would come to thee; and it would, indeed, have all been thine had not that false Don Felix stolen the will away. He took the paper that left all to thee, and thus he won the orphan's gold. But three short days ago, a dreadful crime which he had done was brought to light, and he hath fled. He told me all and bid me give thee, this, thy father's will. [Hagar *gives paper to* Nina.]

Nina. 'Tis strange, most strange. But tell me, Hagar, how didst thou come to know that evil man?

Hagar. I knew him when he came from Italy with thee and thy father years ago. And as I watched thy path through life so I watched his, and thus he learned to trust me. 'Tis thus I gained for thee that wealth so long withheld; and now my work is done. Thou wilt win thy husband's love, and so be happy. God bless thee, gentle lady, and farewell.

Nina. Ah, stay and tell me how can I best show the gratitude I deeply feel. Thou hast brought me wealth and happiness, how can I repay thee?

Hagar. I ask no other joy than that I see in thy fair face. I go now to my own dear land, and we shall not meet again; but old Hagar will remember thee, and pray that life may be one long, bright dream of love with the husband thou hast won. Farewell.

[*Exit* Hagar.

Nina. The clouds have passed away and I am happy now; and the wealth *he* longed for it is mine to give. Oh, Adrian, come back to her thou hast cast aside. [*An arrow bearing a letter is thrown in at the window and falls at her feet*.] What means this letter? Stay, let me see what it may tell me. 'Tis from Adrian. Ah, does an angel watch above me that such joy is mine? [*Opens the letter and reads.*]

Think not to win me back with thy new wealth; I cannot love thee. Be happy with thy gold; it cannot buy the heart of the unhappy

Adrian.

Nina. This from him! No, no, it cannot be; he would not speak such words to me; his wife. Yet, 't is his hand—I must believe—and a deeper darkness gathers round me. No joy, no hope, is left to bind me unto life. If I were gone he might be happy with another. I can never win his love, then why live on to dim his pathway. I will leave my gold to him, for it is worthless now; and when, with her he loves in some fair home, he sends perchance one thought of her who died to free him, I shall be repaid for this last sacrifice. Ah, Hagar, little didst thou think the joy foretold would end so soon, and this thy gift would win for me the rest I long for now [*takes from her bosom the phial and drinks*]. It will soon be past. Now, till sleep steals o'er me, I will send one last word, Adrian, to thee. [*She writes, then sinks upon the couch.*] My heart grows faint, and my eyes are heavy with the last slumber they shall ever know. The poison does its work too soon; but I am done with life, and the soft, sweet sleep of death is holding me. Oh, my husband, may this last deed of mine give thee all the joy it could not bring to her who could only die for thee. Farewell life, farewell love; my latest prayer is for thee, Adrian. [*She lies down and falls gently asleep.*]

CURTAIN

SCENE NINTH

[*Terrace in* Nina's *garden. Enter* Adrian *with letter.*]

Adrian. What means this letter from her hand? 'Twas given me by her servant while she slept. Does she call me home again? Ah, little can she know how fondly now her cold, proud husband longs to fold her in his arms and bless the hour when he lost wealth and won her noble love. [*Opens the letter and reads.*]

> I send thee back the cruel words that have banished all the hopes of happiness with thee. I cannot win thy heart; and this sad truth hath broken mine. And now, upon my dying bed, I leave thee all the wealth that could not win one tender smile for her who pined for it in vain. Thou hast scorned my love, take thou the gold which is worthless to me now. Farewell, my husband; I am faithful to the last, and my lips blessed thee ere they drank the draught that soon will free me from my sorrow, and thee from thy unloved but loving
>
> Nina.

Adrian. My cruel words? What means this? Stay, there is another paper, and it may tell me more. [*Reads* Felix's *forged letter and dashes it down.*] 'Tis false, false as the villain's heart who forged the lie and brought agony like this to that pure, loving heart. Oh, Nina, Nina, now when I so fondly love thee, thou hast been deceived, and died still blessing him thou deemed so cruel and so cold. Oh, that I could but win thee back for one short hour, that I might tell my penitence and my deep sorrow for the grief I have brought thee. Yet, blessed thought, it may not be too late. She slept but one short hour ago, when this was taken from her hand. She may yet linger at the gates of death, and I may call her back to happiness and life once more. Oh, if I may but win this blessing to my heart, my life shall be one prayer of thankfulness for the great boon [*rushes out*].

CURTAIN

145

SCENE TENTH

[Nina's *chamber*. Nina *lies in a deep trance upon her couch.* Adrian *rushes in.*]

Adrian. Nina! Nina! wake, love, it is I thy husband who doth call thee. Oh, can I not win thee back to life now when I have learned to love with all my heart's faith and fondness. [*He kisses her hands and weeps.*] Calm and still she lies, all my tender words cannot awake her, and these bitter tears but fall unheeded and in vain. Was it for this I won that warm young heart,—for this short sorrowing life, this lonely death? Ah, couldst thou see this proud heart humbled now, and these repentant tears that wet thy quiet brow. Nina, wife, oh, wake and tell me I am forgiven! [*Kneels beside her.*]

Nina [*rousing*]. Adrian!

Adrian [*starting up*]. She breathes, she lives, my prayer is heard. 'Tis not too late.

Nina [*still dreaming*]. Methought I was in heaven, for Adrian bent o'er me; the face I loved smiled lovingly upon me, sweet tender words were spoken, and the joy of that short moment well repaid the sorrow I had borne ere that last sleep came. I am happy now for Adrian hath said he loves me.

Adrian. Thy deathlike sleep still hangs about thee, thou art still on earth, and I am here to bring thee joy. Ah, waken and learn thy dream is true. Thy husband loves thee.

Nina. So the sweet vision said, but it hath passed, and this will vanish too. Ah, why hast thou called me back? Life is but a chain that binds me unto sorrow, then let me sleep again and dream that Adrian is true.

Adrian. Nina! Nina! rouse thyself, it is no dream; he hath bent above thee weeping bitter tears and pouring forth his whole heart's love, remorse, and sorrow. His voice hath called thee back to life, and he is here. [Nina *rises and looks wildly about her.*] Here, love, at thy feet seeking thy pardon for the deep wrong he hath done thee, praying thy forgiveness! [*Throws himself at her feet.* Nina *stretches forth her arms, and they embrace with tears of joy.*]

Nina. Adrian, husband, I have naught to pardon. Thou hast won me from the sleep of death, I am thine, thy heart is my home, and I am only happy there.

Adrian. I am unworthy such great happiness. Oh, Nina, thou art the true angel of my life; and thou hast led me on to win a deeper joy than all the wealth of earth could give. I cast thy pure affection by, and sought in selfish sorrow to forget thee; but I could not. Thy dear face shone in all my dreams, and thy voice still lingered in mine ear, imploring me to love thee. Then I returned to find thee drooping like a blighted flower. All loved and honored thee; and I vowed to watch, and, if I found thee true and loving still, to tell thee all, and give my heart to thee forever. I have now won thee, and I love thee, dearest.

Nina. Oh, I am too blest! Life is a flower-strewn path henceforth, where I will gladly journey if thou wilt be my guide; and here upon thy breast, dear love, now smiles the happy wife,—no longer the lonely and unloved one.

[*Tableau.*

CURTAIN

www.ingramcontent.com/pod-product-compliance
Lightning Source LLC
Chambersburg PA
CBHW011512170626
46810CB00009B/3334

* 9 7 8 1 6 3 6 3 7 0 5 0 7 *